THE MOBSTER'S MOLL

The Case of the Dead Husband

BUTTERS PI

RORI BLEU

ROSIE CHAPEL

Ulfire Pty. Ltd.

First printing: 2026
ISBN: 978-1-7644985-4-8 (ebook)
ISBN: 978-1-7644985-5-5 (paperback)

Ulfire Pty. Ltd.
P.O. Box 1481
South Perth
WA 6951
Australia

Cover Design: Rebecca Norman
Images Courtesy: Canva and Deposit Photos
Designed in Canva using appropriate licences.

❀ Formatted with Vellum

THE MOBSTER'S MOLL

Butters P.I.

*"Down these mean streets a man must go who is not himself mean,
who is neither tarnished nor afraid.
The detective must be a complete man and a common man and yet
an unusual man.
He must be, to use a rather weathered phrase, a man of honor—by
instinct, by inevitability, without thought of it, and certainly
without saying it.
He must be the best man in his world and a good enough man for
any world."*

*The Simple Art of Murder
Raymond Chandler*

CHAPTER ONE

1947 - San Francisco

The shrill peal of several telephones ruptured the comfortable hush of the mansion: their, not so melodious, jingles reverberating off tastefully papered walls and down spacious hallways.

Every last one went unanswered.

It was July 4th. My wife and I were relaxing by our newly installed pool, some distance from the main house, and our wonderful, all be they long suffering, staff were enjoying a welcome day off to mark the country's independence.

Swimming laps, I was savoring the tranquility, while Pamela, pretending to read the glossy magazine on her knee watched me over the top of her large sunglasses. I admit, being the object of her admiration boosted my ego and spurred me to continue cutting through the crystal clear water.

I was determined that — despite me celebrating my forty-seventh birthday recently — my darling wife, twelve years my junior, would not find my physical prowess lacking.

I could hear her gloating gleefully, *See, you big lug, refusing to let you retire to become an idle and, doubtlessly, podgy bum was the best wedding present I gave you.*

As I turned at the end of the pool, I noticed her glancing at the martini shaker on the little round table beside her. Even from several feet away, I could tell it was empty and, in the heat of the summer afternoon, the glasses had lost their inviting frostiness.

Shamelessly, she is my wife after all, I stared at Pamela's slender figure as, with efficiency of movement, she balanced everything on the silver tray and sashayed across the lush lawns to the house.

Five years of marriage, and we still behaved like loved-up fools. As a man who once thought the notion of a happily ever after should be consigned to fairy tales, I finally understood the phrase *wedded bliss*. I know, I know, coming from a jaded ex-police officer turned private detective, that sounds sappy and I would not change it for the world.

I grinned to myself. Pamela knew she had caught my eye and was teasing me, attested to by the provocative sway of her hips and shameless wiggle of her cute butt.

Never one to turn down such a blatant offer, I climbed out of the pool, and grabbed the towel I had dropped on the lounger, drying myself off as I chased after her.

When she opened the French doors leading to my office, I heard the faint chime of the telephone, and groaned under my breath. *Who on earth is bothering us today?* I scoured my brain trying to recall whether I had forgotten something important, but came up blank.

Pamela disappeared inside, and I pictured her rolling her eyes at the paperwork and books littering my desk, then felt my face scrunch up in a dismayed grimace, helpless to prevent a pile of documents toppling off when she slid the tray onto the surface.

This is why I designated my study a no go zone, to avoid the possibility of anyone upsetting my system, however inadvertently. I know my beloved, who claims it is a miracle I can find anything, is desperate to tidy up the disaster... her words, but I can put my hands on whatever I need at a moment's notice.

Pamela's cheerful, "Butterfield residence," rang out, but I was not close enough to identify the caller, all I could hear was a faint response.

In a puzzled voice my wife said, "I apologize. We did not expect to be disturbed on this beautiful *holiday*," she emphasized the last word, but obviously did not feel obliged to justify why we had not answered immediately.

The caller spoke and, at Pamela's, "Uh, yes, but he is outside," my heart sank. *Not today.*

Something made Pamela pull the handset away from her head and stare at it in confusion. I could almost see the cogs whirring in her brain. Instinct told me this was not someone calling to invite us to an impromptu Independence Day party. Crossing the threshold into the room, I put a spurt on.

Pamela put the phone back to her ear. "I'm sorry, who is this?"

Whatever the caller said shocked Pamela so much, she sagged against the desk, and her hip jolted the tray. The martini shaker, wedged precariously among the glasses, teetered and tumbled off in a slow arc, splintering into myriad glittering, jagged pieces when it hit the oak floor.

What, under any other circumstances, would have elicited a volley of curses, went unnoticed and, as I dodged shards of glass, I noticed all color leaching from Pamela's face.

Alarmed, I was at her side in a flash. Trying to snap her

out of her shock, I grasped her shoulders and shook her gently. "Pammie, what is it?"

"The call is for you, *Detective* Butterfield. Your ex," Pamela's tone was as devoid of emotion as were her features of her customary smile, but the anger simmering beneath her next words was unmistakable. "Apparently, she needs help and the only person in the whole damn world she could think of contacting is you."

"Stella Fitzhugh?" For a moment, I gawked stupidly between the telephone and Pamela's furious face.

I stretched around her to take the handset, but she slammed it on the desk. The paper and debris strewn about buffered the force somewhat, but Stella surely must have heard it. Berating me in outraged silence, my wife spun on her shapely legs and stormed out.

I heard her heels clicking on the marble stairs, and flinched at the rattle of our bedroom door being shut with extreme force.

I grabbed the handset before it joined the martini shaker on the floor, and ventured, unable to mask my incredulity, "Stella? Is it really you? After all this time?"

"Listen, Jake, this is anything but a social call to revive an old friendship. I've been arrested. You're the only one I could think of to call for help."

"Wait, are you back in San Francisco? You should have called Lou Mazzetti fir—"

"Would you shut up and listen? I am still in Las Vegas. I'm being charged with Red's murder."

"Probably the smartest thing you've done in the last seven years," I muttered loud enough for her to hear.

"Don't be a child, Butters." Her condescension was all too familiar. "No, I did not shoot him, but the idiots here refuse to believe me. Not helped by the fact, the DA is running for office and, presumably, hanging my husband's murder on me guarantees him the governor's mansion. Look, I'm running out of time for this call. Just get here quickly, and put that license *I* organized to good use."

"You know it's only valid in California," my protest was lost to a dial tone, as the call disconnected.

Replacing the handset on the cradle, I looked at the mess on the floor while considering whether my generosity of spirit extended to leaping to the aid of my one-time partner, given the manner of our parting.

Concluding I could, quite easily, leave Stella in the lurch, I also elected to leave the glass where it lay and let the staff earn their keep. Yes, it would be tomorrow but, did I care? Not a single iota.

Self-destruction being my middle name, and hating being on the outs with Pamela, I headed upstairs to our room.

Aware she had, unceremoniously, banged the door shut, I was relieved to find it unlocked. Peering around, I was greeted with the sight of two small suitcases on the bed, an assortment of Pamela's clothes were stuffed into one and she was pulling more from the closet.

Afraid to approach her, I asked sheepishly, "Can we talk first?"

"No... nor do I feel like it. So, button it, and start packing."

"Wait, are you kicking me out?"

"For Chrissakes, Jacob, do you, for one second, imagine I have any intention of letting you go to Vegas to see *that woman* by yourself?"

CHAPTER TWO

According to Rand McNally, it was going to take two days to drive from San Francisco to Las Vegas along Routes 66 and 91. My suggestion to spend the night in Barstow was met with a disgruntled *hmph* from my wife — the first sound she had made since leaving the mansion.

I would not be at all shocked if the sage who first declared that, "Hell has no fury like a woman scorned," had just encountered the equivalent of a jealous Latina with a purple belt in karate... and lost.

Another of my not so brilliant ideas. I should have zipped my lips and kept my eyes on the road.

"This is ludicrous, Jacob Butterfield." Pamela emphasized her point with a chop to my right shoulder. "Why on earth do we need to drive all the way to Las Vegas to save your floozy ex-girlfriend?"

Whack.

"Because *you* were the one who decided to pack," I reminded without glancing sideways.

"Why couldn't she call some gumshoe in Vegas? I'm sure

the bank of phones in the Clark County Jail is full of their phone numbers."

Whack.

My arm was becoming tender, but I figured it was better to let her vent her frustrations on me, than toss her out of the car somewhere along the highway; especially since the Packard Super 6 convertible was registered in Pamela's name only.

These babies were hyped to hit 100 miles per hour. Tempted to see how much juice I could squeeze out of her precious coral blue behemoth, I promised myself to keep it at a comfortable cruising speed of 60.

"Would you trust a number you got from a wall?" I quizzed, reasonably, I thought. "More importantly, it looks like she can't trust anyone else."

"If that's true, and sue me for being skeptical, why didn't she call that lummox Mazzetti? Isn't he the Chief of Police for our fair city?"

At least this time she didn't karate chop me.

"That doesn't do her any good in Vegas, besides the two kinda have a past."

"Christ, don't tell me the three of you—"

"*What?*" I cut her off. "Oh, God no. She was blackmailing him to our mutual benefit."

That slip earned me another *whack.*

"Wow, you just thought about revealing that tidbit? He was your best man at our wedding. No wonder he looked uncomfortable during the toast."

That was the prequel to a long, somewhat acrimonious, and drawn-out conversation which lasted for the next several hours.

All the way to Barstow.

. . .

Needless to state, the night at the motel in Barstow was not peaceful. Our protracted and heated discussion prompted the couple in the adjacent room to pound on the wall. Evidently, we were loud enough to interrupt their lovemaking.

When they threatened to summon management to have us removed, we called it quits — as did our neighbors, because we heard nothing but silence for the rest of the night.

I understood their pique. The anonymity of these out-of-the-way motels, was what attracted a certain calibre of guest. I recalled the hours spent staked out in front of similar *quality* suites, spying on wealthy businessmen giving dick-tation to naive secretaries who were hanging onto the promise of becoming the next Mrs. So-and-So.

Morning brought an uneasy truce. We were tired of bickering, and hungry. The cozy diner alongside the motel provided neutral ground. Tucking into a hearty breakfast, we agreed to act like a respectable couple or, at the very least, professional investigators.

Appetites satiated, we climbed back into the Packard and set off along Route 91, towards America's gambling mecca.

It was slow going for the first part of the drive but, once we hit the vast expanse of the Mojave Desert, I opened up the throttle and, soon, we were cruising at a very acceptable eighty.

Traffic was as sparse as the landscape during the journey to Sin City. For want of a hint of civilization more than anything else, we stopped to refill the car and brave a snack from one of the service stations who struggled to stay in business along this lonely road, while fighting a constant and losing battle against the encroaching desert sand.

Checking my watch, I saw it was nearly time for afternoon visitations at the Clark County Jail. Reasonably full after our sandwiches, we decided lunch could wait, and set off for the jail.

Easing the Packard into one of the designated spaces, we alighted and headed into the security clearance station. The guard demanded to see our identification, who we wanted to meet with, and why.

I flashed my Investigator's License, hoping he would not notice it was issued in California.

"Jacob Butterfield. My associate and I are here to speak with Stella Fitzhu—" I started to explain, which sent the guard in search of the name on his clipboard.

Pamela, in her best, *how dare you demote me to an underling* sneer, "No, Mr. Butterfield, it's Stella *Russo*."

She gave the guard a knowing smile. "You'll have to forgive, Mr. Butterfield. His memory is still hazy since he took a baseball bat to his head."

He arched a quizzical brow at me, which I acknowledged with an apologetic nod, then, using his pencil, directed us into an adjacent room.

"Wait at one of the tables. A matron will bring her in shortly."

I swore I heard him mutter, "If *he's* here to prove her innocence, they might as well gas her now."

Ignoring the slight, we did as he had bidden. It was a soulless room, the fading drab paint seemed deliberately chosen to suck out the minimal light streaming through the small windows. The tables were squat with four chairs around each.

We chose two chairs on the same side, and I took out a notepad, expecting Pamela to chastise me for not introducing her properly. Thankfully, there was no time for her recriminations.

The door on the far side of the visitors' room opened. My gaze shifted to the lithe woman entering escorted by a dowdy prison matron.

Even with her, now bottle-blonde, hair wrapped up in a headscarf, I had no problem recognizing Stella, complete with… to my well-concealed astonishment… her characteristic *Certainly Red* painted lips.

Despite her prison-issue gray dress and canvas deck shoes, she looked as though she had walked off a Hollywood glamour magazine photoshoot.

Instinctively, I rose as she approached the table. Mother Butterfield had taught her son manners.

Without warning, she leaned close to buss my cheek, whispering, "You never change, Butters."

I was unaware of the lipstick smudged she had, unrepentantly, left on my jaw… until Pamela tugged me back to my seat, with a growled, "Down, boy."

"Russo," the matron barked. "No physical contact."

Flippantly dismissing the command, Stella let a measure of vulnerability slip, the legitimacy of which I could not be certain. "Thank God you're here, Jake. There's no one I can trust more—"

Pamela cleared her throat angrily.

Stella's eyes lingered on me, then she looked at Pamela. She smiled cordially. "You must be Pamela Wentworth. It's—"

"*Butterfield*," Pamela corrected.

"Excuse me?" I heard the feigned innocence in Stella's reply. "Oh, yes, how stupid of me. I am sorry for the mistake. Of course it's Butterfield. I must say, your pictures in the papers don't do you justice."

"I… err… thank you…" Pamela's nails dug into my skin as

she draped her hand on my wrist. "Since you've dragged us through the desert to this godforsaken hole, please explain exactly what you expect of *myself and my husband.*"

The inflection Pamela placed on her last words was akin to a slap in the face, but it was like water off a duck's back to Stella who, with typical nonchalance, took no notice. It *did* serve to make her realize, however, she needed Pamela on her side and, in an attempt at appeasement, reached across the table, to pat my wife's arm solicitously, drawing an irate glare from the matron.

Retracting her fingers quickly, my erstwhile partner disclosed the reason for her incarceration, and why she needed me... err... us.

"I did not murder my husband, I swear. Yeah, sure, Red and I fought like cats and dogs, but he usually provided for me..." she finished the sentence on a wink "...kinda like someone else."

I gripped Pamela's hand to keep her from scratching our prospective client's eyes out.

"Go on, Mrs. Russo." I was determined to keep this professional.

My formal address appeared to catch Stella off-guard. "Yes, yes." She collected herself.

Taking a breath, she filled us in on their relationship, "As you might have read in the papers, last year, Red opened a new casino here in Vegas, the Platinum Empire, and was planning to open an adjoining ten-story hotel this year, to offer gamblers the full works, casino and resort all in one. He wanted it to be the first thing you see when you arrive. Towering over everything like some kind of beacon."

"If you drive down the Strip to the intersection of Las Vegas Boulevard and Flamingo Road, which just so happens to be the heart of the city, you'll see the monstrosity." Her derision was not lost on me.

"I'm astounded at how easily he persuaded his investors to plow so many greenbacks into the project, but it's all about the location. Unfortunately, while it looks all shiny on the outside and the first five stories are fully equipped and ready for use, the upper levels are nothing but a shell. Construction kept getting delayed, and permits mysteriously deferred or pulled. When the contractors decided to work, costs were inflated, and supplies…well they just weren't available."

"Wait," I interjected. "If the lower floors are the only ones completed, how was Red murdered in the penthouse?"

"Call him vain. He wanted his throne finished first so he could oversee the project. It also gave him an added measure of privacy because the only way to the penthouse was via the sole fully functional elevator."

"Who had access to that elevator?" Pamela asked, her tone indicating she had heard enough and wanted to pin every-thing on Stella.

"Housekeeping. Those Red had vetted that is. Security," she paused for a moment as though running through the list in her head, "and Aristo Brigmann."

I had tuned Stella out, to focus on what I remembered about the man she had just mentioned.

German born, Aristo's Jewish parents had paid with their lives to smuggle him out of the country when he was twenty, to an uncle of questionable repute in Italy, before Hitler's men got their hands on him, and sent him to Dachau.

After working for said uncle, he was dispatched to the US via Portugal to work for the New York Syndicate, which the US Naval Intelligence was funding to combat Nazi saboteurs and subversives.

His ruthless nature, in addition to his uncle's tutelage in how to juggle accounts ledgers, brought him to the attention of the mob. In particular, Eli Cohen.

If you believed the word on the street, the kid was set up as the Syndicate's accountant and put in direct oversight of the Las Vegas Expansion Project, making him Red Russo's boss.

It was no secret that Brigmann liked the life Vegas offered. Flashy showgirls, stars, cars, jewelry — he wanted it all.

There were also whispers, the ring adorning Brigmann's right pinky once belonged to a Vegas local whom the former found it necessary to *reprimand* for coming up short on a loan payment. A man now lacking his left hand.

That Brigmann had access to Russo's private residence, curdled my palate. Given it appeared the Las Vegas police did not consider him a suspect made the bad taste worse.

"Plus yourself, of course," I heard Pamela contend accusingly, disrupting my thoughts.

"Well, of course," Stella conceded. "Red was my husband, so yeah, I lived there, too."

The pair had a brief stare down, which Pamela won when Stella broke eye contact saying, "Let me tell you what happened that day."

CHAPTER THREE

I cannot deny my former partner knows how to captivate her audience. Pamela and I were transfixed by Stella's version of events.

Later, I praised every God in the existence of the world that firstly, my clever wife had learned shorthand and secondly, had the foresight to make a comprehensive set of notes… which she had transcribed into a juicy murder mystery… putting my scribbled dot points to shame.

In the moment, I confess I barely picked up my pencil. I know, rookie error. Without Pamela, crucial details might have gone unrecorded.

Not a former investigator for nothing, Stella started her recitation well before the actual murder.

You could have heard a pin drop.

Stella's Statement

As documented by Pamela Butterfield, with side notes to clarify certain aspects.

Stella crossed the thinly populated casino floor, carrying a pile of invoice folders and *Past-Due* notices, trying to figure out when in the hell she had become the bookkeeper for this damn money-pit. Made more depressing because it was July Fourth and a Friday to boot. The floor ought to be swimming with gamblers and tourists.

Unfortunately, the dealers twiddling their thumbs behind empty tables outnumbered those earning their keep. She felt her frown deepen when she passed the rows of silent slot machines.

She had heard a particularly nasty rumor about Red ordering several of the slots to be tweaked to payout, in an attempt to drum up business. Regrettably, given no one had tried to substantiate the scuttlebutt by winning, the gamblers must have assumed it was a trick because who in their right mind ever helped the rollers *win?*

Skirting the entertainment stage, where she expected… hoped… to see a huge crowd — it was designed to hold up to five hundred people — there was only a handful of customers.

Currently, the casino could not afford a B-lister, let alone a headliner, reduced to booking acts from the bottom of the barrel. A comedian, who was not funny and believed Vaudeville still existed, along with a singer who was well past her prime, the victim of too many cigarettes and resort buffet tables.

She reached the bank of elevators, grumbling about Red's lack of business acumen.

. . .

Keenly aware of Stella's fastidious account keeping, this had made me chuckle earning matching glares for interrupting.

Tucking the pile of paperwork under one arm, Stella removed the key hanging on a chain around her neck, slid it into the keyhole on the panel, and pressed the button marked PH. A jolt announced the elevator's ascent to the residence she shared with Red, trying not to be unnerved by the creaks and grinds as the car crept upwards.

"I swear if this car crashes to the bottom of the shaft, I'm gonna come back and haunt you, Red," she vowed to her blurry reflection in the doors, adding it to the increasingly long list of miscellaneous teething troubles.

Juddering to a halt, the elevator doors opened to the sound of Red shouting at somebody from his den. The frequency of which was becoming the rule not the exception.

"I'm telling you,' Red's outrage reverberated along the hall. "Someone in this city has it out for me." There was silence while, Stella assumed, he listened to the person on the other end, then, 'No, I'm not wasting either your time or money, sir… and sending the *boy*," the scorn in his voice made his opinion of Brigmann plain, "up here to look at the books won't make this place build itself any faster."

Stella walked to the doorway of his den, wondering whether her husband was about to have a heart attack as he barked, "I don't care what Brigmann is telling you, sir. He's a goddamn liar, and as corrupt as they come."

There was another pause, then Red relented, albeit grudgingly, "Yes, Mr. Cohen, I understand. I'll be expecting him this afterno—" Red's eyes widened, and he glared at the phone before dropping the receiver onto the cradle.

Stella guessed the aforementioned Mr. Cohen was the one and only Eli Cohen who, she knew, was tired of Red's bullshit about the hotel opening being only slightly behind the promised date, and only a little over budget.

Cohen hanging up, combined with the look on Red's face, told Stella how much trouble her husband was in with the Syndicate.

Although unwilling to add to his woes, Stella had no choice and dumped her load on his desk. Hoping to avoid another argument, she infused a placatory note into her voice. "Your morning expense reports, Mr. Russo. Unfortunately, the drywall contractor has pulled his crew, *again*, until his last bill is settled."

Side note: At this point, Jacob bit his lip to prevent what I believed to be a rude snort, apparently — so he explained after we left the jail — because placatory was not a word he would ever associate with Stella. She countered with, "I know, but it was like treading on eggshells."

I continued reading...

Red ripped the file in half. "Doesn't that asshole know who he's dealing with."

"His brother-in-law is the county building inspector, so I don't think he cares, Red," Stella reminded him, exasperated with this repeated conversation.

"Then maybe he should." Red paced the floor. "I have no qualms taking the both of them to Death Valley, smearing them in honey, and staking them to an ant hill."

Stella lost her temper; it was like flogging a dead horse. "What good would that do? You'd just be stuck greasing a whole set of new palms. We both know you don't have the ready cash for that."

Red snarled, "Christ, Stella, some wife you turned out to be. Where is your support? Aren't you supposed to be a genius at pulling victory from the jaws of defeat?"

He threw the papers at her, demanding she produce something to save them…. anything. What did he think she was? A magician?

Side note: Stella shook her head and paused, evidently replaying the scene in her head before adding, "At that moment, I almost felt sorry for him… almost."

I had caught of flicker of something in Stella's eyes at that moment, gone so fast I thought I had imagined it. Unbeknownst to me, Red's crushed expression had reminded her of me... of the day she left. The day she turned her back on me and walked out of my life.

Stella stared off into the distance, her face wan and pinched. I had no idea what was going through her mind but, for a split second, time rewound, and I was running along that platform begging her to stay.

Curiously, while her abrupt departure... abandonment? ... had left me temporarily bereft and adrift — from my perspective, it seemed Fortune had favored me, not Stella. Something I could not have predicted.

Stella lifted her shoulders and schooled her features, muttering bleakly about memories and bad choices.

I did not press for details. Pamela and I only just reached an entente. I was not foolish enough to reignite hostilities.

Back to the account...

Stella was about to explain that she had already tried and come up empty, that he had dug his own grave, and she couldn't help him.

Before she got the chance, Red landed a vicious backhand across her jaw. His diamond wedding ring tore a bloody gash in the corner of her lips. The blow sent her reeling into the wall which also prevented her from landing on her backside.

The coppery taste of blood oozed into her mouth, and she pressed a trembling hand to the laceration, spitting a globule of blood onto Red's prized, nineteenth century, silk Persian rug in front of his desk.

Her hand had fluttered to her mouth, drawing our attention to the scarcely healed cut at the edge of her lip and the bruise marring her cheek.

As when she first told us, her voice lacking any emotion, I felt the same rush of fury and, for the second time, wished Red Russo was alive and well, so I could beat him to death.

With effort, I curbed my anger and concentrated on the words currently jumping around on the page.

. . .

Her eyes narrowed. "If you even think about pulling that stunt again, Carmine Russo—" she warned.

Side Note: Stella explained she called her husband Carmine only when she was angry with him. She preferred to call him Red, mainly because he hated the nickname, which had more to do with his ruddy complexion owing to his heavy drinking, than the russet color of his hair.

"—I swear to the Virgin Mary, I will cut out your heart."

"Haven't you done that already?" Red retorted without batting an eyelid. "I know you want me dead. Truth be told, I'm surprised you and that fucking Brigmann aren't conspiring to knock me off."

She had looked at us with haunted eyes. "I have no idea where he got the idea I hated him. Yes, he annoyed me with his intransigence, but hate him? No, I didn't hate him, although his paranoia, and baseless accusations were sucking the life out of me.

"I tried to talk to him, but he wasn't in the mood, so I decided to leave him to it. He usually wallowed in self-pity for a while, then calmed down and apologized. He always did." She had smiled sadly.

Stella headed to the elevator. Red continued to taunt her. "Don't you dare think of leaving me, Stella. Not until I say it's over. There's no place on earth you can hide from me."

Closing her eyes, she tried to ignore him. As the elevator pinged its arrival, Stella opened them to find herself face-to-face with Aristo Brigmann.

Brigmann flashed a cheesy smile.

Although puking on Brigmann's Italian loafers would give her enormous satisfaction, Stella made do with rolling her eyes and stepping to one side to allow the accountant to pass.

Brigmann had other ideas. "Well, if it isn't the charming and captivating Mrs. Russo. I hope the day finds you well."

Deadpan, Stella replied, "It finds me. Now, if you'll excuse me, Mr. Brigmann—"

The man's smile never faltered as he corrected, "Please, it's Aristo. Mr. Brigmann sounds far too... stuffy between friends."

Wishing to be anywhere but here, especially since her cheek was throbbing, she snapped, "I'm sorry, Mr. Brigmann, but I'm not feeling particularly friendly today..." imagining a shark chomping the repulsive man into bite-sized pieces then swallowing the lot, "...so, I'll leave you to take care of business with Red."

"Ahh, you must spare a few moments to join us. You are just as vital to the success of this project as your husband."

It sounded like a warning, and before Stella could react, Brigmann led her back to Red's office, where he shoveled her into a chair, and started to lower the blackout curtains.

Side Note: Stella looked at us both and said, "I confess, this alarmed me."

"*Alarmed* you? Understatement of the year. It would terrify me," Jacob exclaimed as he caught my eye. The temperature in the room seemed to drop and I gripped his hand. We both knew what was coming but, like a runaway train, we couldn't stop it.

Stella continued as though Jacob hadn't interrupted.

. . .

Red glanced up from the paperwork he was reorganizing after his childish tirade to ask, "Why are you closing my drapes, Brigmann, and what is she doing here?"

"Ah, Red, why so hostile, especially in front of your gracious spouse?" Brigmann's sounded insincere. "I was hoping to convince Stella here to serve as hostess."

He took a flask from his inner pocket. "Top shelf stuff, Stella, trust me. Would you mind?"

Reluctantly, Stella acquiesced and, taking the flask, used the contents to concoct three highballs, assuming the alcohol to be whiskey.

Side Note: Stella said to us, "As with the drapes, this should have raised a red flag, but it didn't. I just assumed it was his favorite whiskey. He is very particular about his spirits. Even when I picked up the glasses, and noticed the liquid appeared slightly cloudy, I had no reason to question him."

Her mouth contorted briefly. "Hindsight is a wonderful thing.

Brigmann answered Red's question, "As for the drapes, if you must know, the sunlight is giving me a migraine."

"And that's my problem, why?" Red snapped.

Ignoring Red, Brigmann ensured the sun was blocked out, then stooped to retrieve one of the unpaid accounts from the floor, beating Red to it.

Reading the invoice, Brigmann shook his head disapprovingly, then handed it to Red.

Putting the drinks on Red's desk, Stella resumed her seat. Brigmann was not the only person with a migraine brewing;

this entire day had become one long headache. Stella sipped her drink, absently, exhaustion prowling.

Red snatched the proffered sheet and returned to his desk. Avoiding Brigmann's gaze, he said, "Why are you here so soon? I wasn't expecting you until later this afternoon."

"I was fortunate to procure a room in the *yet-to-be-completed* Platinum Hotel. When Eli…" few people referred to the mob boss so casually. Most addressed him as Mr. Cohen. Even then, depending on his mood, doing so might be considered disrespectful and earn the person a bullet to the head… "called my room and asked me to check the books, I came right up.

"While I appreciate you making sure the paperwork would be awaiting my arrival, I can assure you it was not necessary. I receive a duplicate of everything which passes through your office."

Brigmann moved behind Stella and placed his hands on her shoulders. His touch made her want to vomit, but she was unable to escape it.

"Let's say a little bird keeps an eye on you and relays information to me."

Suspecting Brigmann was referring to Stella, Red glowered at her in tacit but infuriated accusation and before she could refute it, all the lights went out.

I did not need Pamela's notes for the last part of Stella's account. It was indelibly engraved into my mind.

"Two shots were fired in quick succession, the muzzle blast damn near blinded me, and the blowback from the barrel burning my cheek and hand. There was a shocked silence, then all hell broke loose.

"I felt something hot and heavy drop into my lap. I grabbed it at the same moment as the lights came back on. Shit, Butters, it was .32, still smoking. I can still smell the acrid odor." White-faced, she shuddered.

"There was a terrible ringing in my right ear leaving me pretty much deaf, but I heard a muffled shriek. I looked for the source. The scene was surreal, like a waking nightmare.

I saw a woman screaming hysterically. I didn't recognize her, but she was wearing a housekeeper's uniform. I have no clue where she came from, but given Red could not keep it in his pants, probably the bedroom.

"Everything was blurry, and I wanted Red to help me. I squinted at his desk, and it looked like he was taking a nap, using the financial statements as a pillow. This irked me. I was the one who was tired not him.

"Then I realized, there was something wrong with the picture. His eyes were open, and the papers seemed to be blotting something red. At first, I thought he must have spilled a bottle of ink, God knows we were drowning in it, then it came to me. It was blood.

"I barely had time to process this when I heard the click of a pistol's hammer behind me. I tried to turn my head but couldn't because a nickel-plated .45 was pressed hard against my ear. It was Brigmann, the bastard." She spat his name in utter contempt.

"He ordered the frantic housekeeper to, 'Shut up and call the cops. She just killed her husband.' I couldn't believe it, how could I shoot Red? I don't have a... I remembered the gun in my hand.

"Brigmann leaned close and warned, 'Don't know what was going on in that pretty head of yours, Russo, but if you think you can pin this on me, you're sadly mistaken. What a shame. An argument which got out of hand. Anyone who had cause to go higher than the fifth floor, construction workers, staff, could hear you two haranguing each other.'

"He smiled at me. The louse actually smiled at me. Well, if you can call that evil smirk a smile."

Clark County Jail

She stopped speaking, and there was a long silence as the stark surrounds of the visitors' room came back into focus. Stella's shoulders slumped in defeat. No fool, she knew how improbable it sounded.

"That's the truth, the whole truth, and nothing but the truth," her attempt at levity fell short, ruined by her pale face and the dread lurking in her eyes. "My fingerprints are all over the gun. The paraffin test, of course, came back positive, as if there was ever any doubt," she concluded bitterly. "Aristo Brigmann shot Red and left me to take the fall."

Pamela looked at me, her disbelief palpable. Even I was having a hard time swallowing this story.

This was not wasted on Stella. Her eyes widened as it dawned on her that the only two people who might save her were questioning her innocence.

"Look, Jake, you know me," she pleaded. "Yeah, I can run a good scam, and an even better extortion racket but I could never murder anybody. The fact you're still alive after what happened between us should be proof enough. Please, I need your help."

I evaluated her statement. Outlandish — definitely... buuuuut... she was right, murder was not her métier. Yeah, I know, French. What can I say? I am a man of hidden talents. Also, her description of events was so far-fetched as to be ludicrous. No one would be stupid enough to make up such an implausible story and expect anyone to believe it.

Seconds ticked by, and Stella was all but squirming in her panic, until I took pity on her. "Fine, but if I find the faintest shred of evidence you're guilty, I'll make sure they bury you in the Nevada State Prison."

Stella sagged with relief, and she nodded, then dared ask another question. One which utterly flabbergasted Pamela.

"Can you post my bond, as well?"

CHAPTER FOUR

Pamela clung to the last threads of silent treatment until we climbed into the Packard. No sooner had I put the car in reverse, than she aired her feelings… at a volume, I am sure, even Stella, no matter how deep in the jail they had confined her, must have heard.

"Let me get this straight, Jacob Butterfield, not only are we in this God-awful town for *your* former girlfriend—"

"In my defense, it was *your idea* to come," I parried without thinking.

"Shut up. I'm not done. You say another word, and I'll demonstrate the newest move, Sensei taught me and toss your sorry ass out of this convertible.

She knew me well. I considered pointing out the danger of physically ejecting the driver from a moving vehicle, then thought better of it.

"*And…*" she railed, "*you* have the unmitigated gall to agree to spend *my* money—"

"I thought it was our money?" Slipped out before I could stop it. *Playing with fire again, Butters,* my inner-self remonstrated in exasperation.

Which was, unsurprisingly, met with another blistering, "Shut up," this time accompanied by a thump to my shoulder.

With an aggrieved humph, she crossed her arms, glared out of the passenger side window, and growled, "Get a bail bondsman for her. If she skips town, which I am sure she will, I prefer to lose the ten thousand surety than the entire bond."

Having that much money at your disposal comes with problems only the rich understand, I mused... with the only the vaguest hint of cynicism, honest!

"That way, someone else will be responsible for dragging her keister back here."

She paused to assess what lay ahead of us. "Never mind that, until Monday, when the banks and courthouse are open, she's stuck in jail, and we are prisoners in this town." She craned her neck to check our route. "Where are we going anyway?'

Suitably chastened, I replied, "The Platinum Empire Hotel."

Stella had recommended this while Pamela was preparing to leave and had not heard. She had also comped us a free room; an unheard-of luxury except for the high rollers.

She had assured me, despite still being under construction, those areas of the hotel designated as complete were habitable. Plus, it meant we did not have to fabricate a pretext to search the place.

We drew up at the entrance, expecting to find a valet or two to park our car, but there was no one manning the stand. After the third or fourth blare of the horn, a gangling youth with slicked back hair and sunglasses popped out of the hotel.

"Don't flip your wig, Pops, I'm coming," the kid groused at being compelled to brave the oppressive heat.

He opened Pamela's door with a smile as greasy as his hair. Once she alighted, he shut her door and met me at the trunk.

"You have a reservation?" he queried. "Otherwise, it's fifty cents to park this thing."

"I don't have a reservation, per se."

"Hmmm. Not good." He frowned. "It is the holiday weekend, if you'd forgotten."

Getting insulted by this kid was pissing me off. "I am well aware of that, thank you."

"Tell ya what, for a buck, let them know Hank vouched for you, and that everything is copacetic. I guarantee a room will be open for you, maybe even the penthouse, considering it ain't being used right now."

That this kid might know something useful, piqued my interest. Unfortunately, before I could press him for details, he had lifted the suitcases out of the trunk, handed them to me, then jumped into the front seat and burned the rubber off my tires. The cloud he left made me wonder whether he was planning to park the Packard in Los Angeles.

I looked for Pamela, to see her marching into the hotel. Hefting the luggage, I hurried to catch up.

At the sound of our footsteps in the empty lobby, the desk clerk looked up from her magazine.

"You have reservations?" she greeted us in a softly accented voice.

Pamela ushered me forward. "We don't have reservations, but Stella Russo—"

The girl's eyes widened.

"—was supposed to have reserved a room for the Butter-fields. Mr. and Mrs."

"I'm not sure she could. Currently, she's…" she stopped short of revealing Stella was under arrest. "Please allow me to get the hotel manager."

"And the concierge," Pamela interjected.

"Ma'am?" The command caught the clerk off guard.

Doubtless, she supposed Pamela had requested the concierge in case we were turned away. The kid outside was right, it was the holiday weekend, and we had no idea how busy the hotel was.

The girl disappeared through a doorway to an adjoining office, reemerging almost immediately behind a well-dressed man in a tuxedo on which was pinned a shiny gold name tag identifying him as Richard Stedman, Manager.

Mr. Stedman introduced himself and, with what sounded like a sigh of resignation, contemplated us, before offering what I anticipated to be his rehearsed excuse, explaining why he could not possibly comply with our request.

His next words were, therefore, unexpected. "Mrs. Russo told us to expect you when she was…" he too sought a polite phrase "…detained. I have you on the fifth floor. There is only one other guest on that level, which ought to afford you the privacy you are likely to require."

I flashed my ID. "Then you are aware of the reason for our visit."

"Yes, sir. Although, if you need to investigate areas currently off limits to the public, I will need to get permission first."

"Fair enough," I acknowledged. We could explore most of this place without anyone noticing. I had spent the better part of the last decade perfecting the art. "We would like to examine the penthouse."

"The police are still gathering evidence. It is an active crime scene," the manager cautioned.

"We understand and would never presume to interfere." I replied at the same time as my wife gave me her, *When did that stop you,* look.

"I will arrange access for you," the manager assured us.

He took it upon himself to check us in. Handing us the key, he motioned to one of the bellhops to carry our luggage.

Pamela refused to move. In fact, I thought I saw her stamp her foot. "Aren't the two of you forgetting something?"

The manager and I looked at each other as though we had been asked the $64,000 question and had no clue as to the answer.

"The concierge? If we are going to be here for the weekend, I want tickets to some shows. Lena Horne is performing at the Flamingo, and so is Jimmy Durante. Two tickets to each would be appreciated and make sure to put them on Mrs. Russo's account."

The concierge was standing to one side, awaiting his introduction. Pamela's request prompted him to break protocol. "I'm sorry, ma'am, but those are some of the hottest tickets in the city. I mean we have other options which are equally entertaining."

Pamela arched one eyebrow at the man. Beads of sweat pebbled on his forehead at the intensity of her stare.

Before she heaped contempt on the poor guy for doing his job, I intervened, "Sweetheart, I'm sure this gentleman will do everything in his power to fulfill your request, even if he has to create the tickets himself with a box of wax crayons. Now, how about we freshen up in our room and find something to eat? I hear the steakhouses here are second to none," I tempted.

Pamela's expression lit up for the first time since we

arrived in Las Vegas. She was a lot like me in that regard — steak made everything better.

"Jacob, you do have the best suggestions. I am famished." She beamed.

I hid my relief at this shameless diversionary tactic, and glanced at the concierge, who scrambled to his podium to retrieve tickets for free steak dinners at a joint on the Strip, which vowed to be the best place in Nevada. If I was to guess… whatever tickets he might produce would get the same billing.

Handing them over, he informed us proudly, "Do not be concerned, Mrs. Butterfield. I shall see about getting those tickets. It is too late for this evening's show…" which elicited an instant moue of disapproval from my wife, "…let me work my magic."

Pamela extended her hand to the concierge who grasped her fingers and bowed as though she was royalty, which she was in an American sense.

Over her shoulder, she beckoned, "Come on, Jacob, let's get changed and enjoy the city.

Our suitcases deposited in Room 501, the bellhop tipped generously for his work, with promises of more if he heard anything which could assist our investigation, we descended to the lobby and out onto the Strip.

Las Vegas was bustling with new construction. Hotels and casinos were springing up like weeds. The majority, in far better condition than our current residence.

On the way to redeeming our free meals, we stopped at a casino called the Gold Bar. Its doors were propped open like the jaws of a hungry beast ready to pounce on any misguided individuals who believed they could tame it… however erroneously.

Out of the blazing heat, which we discovered later was on a record-breaking run of hundred-plus temperatures, the frigid interior — a result of overworked air conditioning — came as a shock.

Noting the number of people here compared with the Platinum Casino, I nudged Pamela and directed her to a crap table, where a twenty-something redhead was on a particularly lucky streak.

We watched her roll sevens, elevens, and match points. Next to her stood a distinguished gentleman, about twice her age who, occasionally, whispered something to her before she rolled again.

Slipping from Pamela's side, I wandered across to him.

"Looks like your girl is on good form," I commented.

"You with the casino?" he asked. "'Cause I already had numerous words with the pit boss."

"No, I am just a curious bystander. I've never seen anybody hit like this girl."

"Neither have I," he admitted. "Would you believe me if I told you I met her last night?"

"And now she has you bankrolling her?"

"How could I not? It is amusing to watch her play. I've watched the casino switch out dice on her about ten times. Dealers, I lost track of how many she went through, don't forget, though. They even tried to move her from table to table to break her streak."

"What's her trick?" I ventured.

"Beats me, and I've been gambling for most of my life. The only consistent thing is the size of the bet. Never too greedy and, if anyone matches her bets, she cashes in."

"How much are you up?"

"About fifteen grand. I'm pretty sure the casino is ready to kick her out. We'll just move on to the next place."

"Have you considered playing at the Platinum Empire's casino?"

For a split second, my question silenced him. Staring at me incredulously, he expostulated, "Why would I shell out money where every wheel is probably rigged, and the dice are loaded. 'Sides, who wants to be in debt to the mob? I heard the place has blown its budget by like a million bucks, and certain people are not happy, not helped by the fact, the owner was just murdered by his wife"

"How did you know that?"

"The murder? Vegas is still a small town. People talk."

His meal ticket spoke to him in undertones, nodding at the burly men in suits approaching.

"Collect the chips and cash them in. I'll slow them down."

She brushed a kiss to his cheek and vanished into the crowd.

He said, "If you will excuse me, I need to have a conversation with these apes."

I watched as Security manhandled my new friend out. Through the glass doors, I spotted a little red sports car, the same redhead behind the wheel, waiting for him, her scarf billowing in the hot breeze.

Mr. Money Bags' opinion was reiterated by some of the other gamblers willing to talk.

Over steaks at the restaurant, Pamela and I discussed what we had learned — very little.

After finishing the meal, which I had to admit was better than expected, we strolled back to the Platinum and its pool.

Entering the lobby, I spotted the concierge waving us to his stand. Triumphantly, he brandished tickets for the two shows Pamela wanted to see.

"Thank you for this," Pamela accepted the tickets with delight. "You are certainly a man of your word." That she did not ask how he had managed such a feat, rather took the wind out his sails, but any hint of peevishness abated when Pamela bestowed on him her sweetest smile.

For the time being, our weekend was set.

CHAPTER FIVE

A weekend spent *investigating* the surrounding casinos and restaurants, meant Pamela faced Monday in a much better mood.

The concierge at the Platinum Empire had not failed us on the quality of the tickets he was able to finagle, which also included backstage passes to meet Miss Horne after her concert.

By the end of the night, Pammie and Lennie, as they decided to call each other, had swapped private phone numbers and made plans to have the singer spend Halloween with us.

I have learned never to discount my wife's ability to schmooze people... no matter who they are.

Our frivolity came to an end with the sunrise. It was time to earn our fee.

During breakfast at the hotel where the food was passable, but not somewhere Michelin would squander one of its famous stars, we mapped out our strategy for the day.

We decided to rent another car so we could achieve twice as much. Unfortunately, I did not end up with the stylish Packard. Pamela called dibs, leaving me with a 1934 Studebaker President. It was comfortable enough but lacked finesse.

Pamela had contacted her accountant to arrange for a ten-thousand dollar check to be wired to the local Western Union office.

While she was occupied with the monetary aspect of things, I took the opportunity to introduce myself to the local homicide detectives.

I was required to cool my heels in the lobby, waiting for the desk sergeant to contact the detectives in charge of Red's murder.

An eternity and a half later, a man came in munching a sandwich. Given the thickness of his five o'clock shadow, at ten in the morning, I surmised any personal time since the shooting was non-existent.

Finishing his snack, he stuffed the wax paper into a trash can, brushed the crumbs from his fingers, and greeted me.

"Name's Harrington, Homicide. I understand you have some questions about a case I am working on." He looked me up and down. "How about we start out by finding out who you are."

I pulled out my PI credentials and braced myself for the usual bullshit, while conceding that when I had been in this same position, I would not have expected anything less.

"Jacob Butterfield. San Francisco Private Investigator."

"Hate to tell you, Butterfield, that license and a nickel might get you a cup of coffee here in Vegas but not much else."

Having that pointed out was getting really tiresome.

Ignoring the gibe, I pressed on as though I was standing on Fisherman's Wharf, grilling a potential suspect. "Tell me, Harrington, what makes you think the Russo woman killed her husband?"

The directness of the question brought a smirk to his stubbly face. "Does a pair of witnesses in the room at the time help clarify? Both of whom will testify to overhearing the *loving couple* argue like cats and dogs."

"Doesn't mean she murdered him."

"You're gonna play dumb on this, huh, Butterfield. We have her fingerprints all over the murder weapon."

"Nobody else's?"

"Only the Russo dame's."

"How about the bullets and the magazine? Did you dust those as well?"

Harrington flinched.

I guessed, in his investigative zeal to close the case, the homicide detective had overlooked the most basic of all forensic rules… dust everything.

"Doesn't matter. Her prints are on the grip and the trigger, and she looked like she was trying to bathe herself in the pistol's blowback."

"A little too convenient, don't ya think?"

"Sometimes, we get lucky, Butterfield. Unlike the big cities in Cali, out here in the desert, luck and intuition is our biggest ally. Besides, if the District Attorney is satisfied we have enough evidence for a conviction, who am I to disagree?

"I do not wish to appear rude, but I have neither the time

nor the inclination to continue this discussion. Before you find yourself in trouble in our fair city, I recommend you take your *Dick Tracy ID* and yourself back to Frisco. You're not welcome here."

"That's a shame. I was considering retiring to Vegas," I wise-cracked.

Harrington's reply was to curl his lip in disdain and walk away.

Learning the Las Vegas Police Department was as inept as the cops back home, I decided to see whether Pamela's luck was better at the Platinum.

As I entered the lobby, I heard, "Page for Mr. Butterfield," and saw one of the smartly dressed bellhops searching for me.

He repeated, "Page for Mr. Jacob Butterfield."

I raised my hand in acknowledgement, for all the world as though this was a regular occurrence, despite it being a first. "Here, son."

Hurrying over, the bellhop held out a silver tray on which lay a folded note. I took it, but the empty tray remained extended in my direction and my faux pas hit me as smartly as a palm to the forehead.

Digging in my pocket, I produced a couple of quarters and dropped them on the platter. Evidently, everything in Vegas required a tip.

"More expenses for Stella," I quipped as I opened the note.

It was from Pamela; time stamped twenty minutes ago.

Meet us at the courthouse 1 PM sharp. Look professional.

"Look professional?" I chided, rereading the terse note.

"Does she not know Jacob Butterfield Esquire is the epitome of professionalism."

I guessed it was more a request to behave in an exemplary manner around Stella, than how I dressed. Either way, I would be all business.

Predictably, despite arriving ten minutes early, I found my wife pacing up and down the sidewalk in front of the Clark County Courthouse, glancing at her watch impatiently, and scanning the parking lot.

Rolling the Studebaker into a conveniently close spot, I heard her jeer, "Did you get lost along the way, Butters?"

I quelled the urge to slam the car door shut in indignation and, tempting fate, remarked mildly, "Where's the fire? I reckon there's time to grab lunch if you fancy a bite. What's so important you had to drag me away from a refreshing dip in the pool?"

I saw her pivot in her stilettos and march toward the courthouse entrance, her explanation hanging in the air. "Bailing your murderous girlfriend out of jail wasn't as easy as posting a bond. Seems the county isn't too keen on letting her walk, so now, we have to involve a lawyer."

Inside, she faced me. What she said next made me wince.

"I had Baxter flown out on a private charter."

Baxter Nichols was the Wentworth family's personal lawyer. He had represented Pamela in her contentious battle with her sister regarding their inheritance.

Legal matters aside, the man hated me, deeming me unworthy to stand in Pamela's shadow, never mind marry her.

Unbeknownst to me, my beloved had gone behind my

back and contacted him during the weekend, summoning him to serve as Stella's legal representation to bail her out.

On cue, the lawyer appeared. He did not waste time with pleasantries. We were well past such meaningless niceties.

"Tell me, Butterfield," he asked. "Is your girlfriend likely to bolt and disappear into the desert leaving Pamela in danger of losing her surety?"

It was one thing for Pamela to snipe about Stella being my girlfriend, but this ass had no right.

"First, I have no ties to Mrs. Russo besides being old acquaintances." I saw Pamela's jaw tighten at the admission. "Second, the Stella I knew would never consider leaving somebody willing to help her, on the hook."

The lawyer rolled his eyes, making it clear he doubted Stella's credibility. "Fine, the judge is willing to hear you advocate for her release at one-thirty. Please, remember you will be under oath. Try not to perjure yourself too much."

"I have no need to, Nichols, of that I can assure you."

Turns out, I had no need to testify. In spite of my misgivings about Nichols, from the moment he introduced himself as, "Baxter Nichols, from the law firm of Nichols, Nichols, and McKee, San Francisco, California, here to represent Mrs. Stella Russo," his legal prowess proved to be formidable.

In less than fifteen minutes, Lincoln Devereux, the venerable District Attorney for Clark County, and probable future governor of Nevada, was reduced to an angry, blustering fool by Stella's legal counsel.

"Eugene." Devereux stormed to the bench, to address the presiding judge with complete lack of etiquette. "Surely, you cannot consider permitting that killer..." theatrically, he jabbed a finger at Stella.

Stella played the innocently accused with consummate skill. Her hands folded on her lap neatly, her doe-like gaze giving the impression she was struggling to comprehend the proceedings.

"...to walk freely on the streets of Las Vegas. I guarantee she will kill again."

Nichols rose from his chair. In a measured tone, he said, "Your Honor, we both know, the laundry list of objections I could file against the DA for his histrionics, is unnecessary. While, it is true, my client has a record of minor crimes, they occurred in her youth, and were either dropped, plea bargained down to fines, or, at worst, resulted in short probations."

I always suspected Stella had a questionable past but preferred not to delve too deeply when we were together. *What the eye doesn't see, and all that.*

"At no time did she present a flight risk," Nichols concluded. "Similarly, although I am not, at present, seeking a dismissal for judicial misconduct by the District Attorney's Office and the Las Vegas Police Department, I do respectfully request that the court observe the bail the county set originally. I have a local bondsman, licensed and insured, present in court to secure the bail."

"There were gangsters involved here, Eugene," Devereux argued.

The gavel banged down, silencing the infuriated District Attorney,

"That's Judge Sanders to you, Mr. Devereux," the judge reminded. "One more outburst from you, and you'll find yourself in contempt of court. I don't think your voters would look on your inability to maintain decorum during these proceedings, favorably.

"As for you, Mrs. Russo," Sanders eyed Stella. "I do not care for the class of individuals with whom you associated previously. It is obvious these two, prepared to vouch for your character, are of a higher caliber, are genuinely concerned for you, and will ensure you do not skip future court dates.

"That said, Mrs. Russo, make no mistake. *One* missed hearing, no matter the reason, up to and including your death, will see your bond revoked and the surety forfeited. A bench warrant for your arrest will be issued at that juncture. Am I clear?"

Demurely, Stella answered, "Yes, Your Honor."

"Fine." He banged his gavel again. "See the clerk."

We gathered outside the courtroom to plan our next move.

Nichols advised Pamela that he needed to, "get back to the office."

"Thank you, Baxter. I understand and appreciate you coming on such short notice. I instructed the pilot to wait for you at the airport."

"A treasure as always, my dear."

I wanted to knock him into next week for flirting with my wife right in front of me.

"Call me when you next wish to discuss Mrs. Russo's case, or any more pressing matters such as amending your will or filing for a divorce."

He sent me a calculating look and took his leave.

CHAPTER SIX

Deciding how to return to the hotel became a game of musical car seats.

When Stella suggested she take a cab to the Platinum Empire, I offered to give her a lift. Pamela rejected both ideas and ordered our client to get into the Packard.

I let the women take the lead, which was a good thing. No sooner had they driven off, than a black, late model Ford Deluxe peeled out behind them.

Evidently, they had not seen me climb into the Studebaker, which was fortuitous because now the pursuers were being tailed.

Whoever these jokers were, they must have skipped the class on trailing a suspect covertly because even Pamela spotted them after a couple of blocks. My wife was, had always been, a quick study when it came to cloak and dagger stuff.

She took several right and left turns at random intervals to verify her assumption.

Back on the Boulevard, she accelerated, pulling a few cars

ahead, cutting off a brown Dodge, which earned her a blare of the horn from the aggrieved driver.

Seeing the Ford pull in behind the Dodge, I slipped alongside and cranked my wheel to the left, trying to cut them off. Brakes squealed and horns honked.

Taking avoiding action, the Ford ended up on the sidewalk, sending tourists scattering in all directions. Bound and determined not to let them get away, I followed.

The two cars shuddered as we bounced back onto the road, speeding toward the city limits. I saw the passenger climb into the rear seat and roll down the window.

A .38 revolver poked its ugly snout through the gap and took aim. The car bucked and the two rounds went wild, one smashing my driver's side mirror.

So much for my deposit on the rental.

The second pierced the windshield to embed itself in the front passenger seat. I sent up a prayer of thanks for Pamela's insistence that Stella ride with her.

Knowing I was out a substantial amount of money, I returned fire. My first shot blew out the back window of an innocent Oldsmobile parked at the curb. I hoped it was unoccupied.

The second shot was lucky, and hit the driver's side rear tire, causing it to fishtail and career into a traffic light. The front grille wrapped around the pole launching the driver through the windshield. I doubted he could survive the impact.

The gunman in the backseat crawled out of the vehicle and collapsed onto the ground. He blinked to see my pistol pointed at him.

"Who are you?" I demanded. "Why were you following my wife?"

His only answer was a defiant, "Screw you, gumshoe."

Before I could interrogate the bastard *properly*, meaning

pistol whipping him senseless until he begged to spill the beans, the Vegas police bore down on us in full force.

Just like San Francisco's finest. Nowhere to be seen when you need them but, as if by magic, they appear after the fact.

Sure enough, the first detective on scene was the very same Detective Harrington from this morning.

"For Chrissakes, Butterfield," he exclaimed, examining the wreckage. "Did I not tell you to stay out of trouble in *my* city? Here you are three hours later, one dead motorist hanging out of his windshield and a second about to head to the hospital."

Pamela and Stella had caught up to us and leaped out of the Packard. My wife, overhearing the cop berate me, intervened heatedly, "He saved our lives, *sir*," spitting the last word. "I assure you, if he had not acted so quickly, those two hoodlums would have kidnapped us and buried our remains in the desert."

One of the many things I loved about Pamela was her flare for the dramatic.

Pamela's rebuke forced Harrington to back down, though he felt inclined to inform me, "I need your revolver, Butterfield, until this matter is resolved. Do not dare think of leaving Vegas until I say so."

"First you tell me to go, and now you can't stand the thought. Should I feel flattered?"

"Your former partner told me you were nothing but trouble."

"Ahhh, you talked to Lou this morning. How is the good captain?" I asked, knowing I would have done the same had our roles been reversed.

"Louis Mazzetti?" We both turned to see the broad smile on Stella's blood red lips. "I do hope you sent him my blessings as well, detective. I miss him."

Harrington glared at me. "Just give me your damn gun and get out of my sight."

I did as he bade, making sure to keep the one in my ankle holster.

Hey, so sue me... I gave him what he asked for.

Once the forensic guys had photographed the damage to the Studebaker, giving us the customary cracks about the rental company not being happy, we returned said automobile.

The expression on the agent's face when he met us in the parking lot was priceless.

"What did you do to our beautiful Studebaker? It was pristine when you checked it out this morning. Now look at it," he bleated, examining the shattered windshield, then noticed the hole in the back of the passenger seat.

Circling the vehicle, he found… or, rather, did not find… the missing driver's side mirror.

"Th-this is unacceptable," he stammered, fighting to retain his composure.

"Come now, sir," I tried to soothe him with my usual charm. "It's nothing a good buffing won't fix."

"A good buffing? Are you insane? How do I buff out a shattered windshield or a missing mirror?" Wrath flared in his eyes. "Do not move while I figure out how much damage you have wrought on this poor car."

By the time the agent had found every little ding and scratch ever inflicted during the Studebaker's thirteen-year life… a good hour later… Pamela had reached her limit. As is the habit of the rich, she slapped her checkbook on his desk and started filling it out, demanding, "Just sell me the jalopy, and don't bother jacking up the price."

The ink was scarcely dry on the check before he had the audacity to offer his garage to repair the car. Trying to avoid another hassle, Pamela agreed… with a blunt proviso, "If you think you're about to screw me over, I'll make sure you meet my family's legal team."

That's how I ended up with an automobile I did not want.

If I had any doubts the two gorillas we ran into earlier were hired guns, the nervous manager who met us outside the Platinum's entrance dispelled them. Avoiding eye-contact, Richard Stedman greeted Stella, "Mrs. Russo, it is good to see you."

"Yes, yes, Richard, it's good to see you, too. If you will excuse me, I must go up to my suite to take a—"

"I'm afraid the police have cordoned off the penthouse. I can't let you up there."

"Then, check me into one of the open rooms. I don't care if it's one of the half-finished suites, as long as the tub is plumbed in."

"Mrs. Russo, you know as well as I, that is a health code violation."

"Richard, we both know, the majority of the construction here is not up to code. Unless you want me to go to the papers with that little tidbit, I suggest you give me a room, now."

"A-Allow me to page Mr. Brigmann—" Richard started.

"Brigmann? What does that pencil pusher have to do with this?"

"With Mr. Russo being…" the manager stumbled for a suitable word, "…indisposed, Mr. Brigmann volunteered to step in and serve in his stead."

"Richard, you do realize, *I* am the co-partner in this little venture," Stella reminded tartly.

"I don't know anything about the status of upper management at this point, Mrs. Russo," he tried to deflect the conversation.

"Then perhaps you should get him down here," Stella's dulcet tones belied the storm clouds gathering in her eyes.

Pamela and I traded glances. Even my wife was concerned about Stella's state of mind, which was stretched tighter than a violin string. If it snapped, the repercussions would be catastrophic.

I knew what Pamela was thinking even before she said anything. While she could be an ice princess at times, she still possessed a heart of gold.

"Jacob, I think we should ask her—"

I held my hand up to stop her. "Not until we know for sure, my love."

It took Brigmann some time to make his appearance. I made no comment to my companions when I saw the woman in the large floppy hat and dark glasses, who followed him out of the elevator, but my senses went on high alert. The couple were sharing a laugh, and she had the moxie to brush a kiss to his cheek, removing the lipstick smudge with her thumb.

That little love scene was seared into my memory.

I remembered Stella saying, a mysterious housekeeper had appeared during the shooting, causing my overly suspicious nature to posit this might be the same woman.

The pair separated and headed in opposite directions, but not before Brigmann noticed me watching them.

His demeanor hardened visibly as he approached, and

greeted Stella less than civilly, "I'm astonished to see you out of jail, let alone here."

"Yeah, and I'm afraid to tell you, your hired idiots were no match for my Private Dick," Stella retorted with a wry grin, much to the chagrin of my wife, though she let it slide.

"I have no idea what you're talking about, Mrs. Russo."

"No matter. Just tell Stedman to rent me a room so I can get the prison stink off of me."

He flipped the guest register around and paged through it for a moment. "No can do, appears we are fully booked. Must be a convention or something. Besides, I think under the circumstances, having you in this hotel would not be prudent. An assessment shared by the *majority* investors."

Meaning the Eastern Syndicate in general and, no doubt, Eli Cohen in particular.

Pamela broke in., "Do you have a trundle bed available?"

Stedman answered, "Yes, but I do not know how that would be helpful. She cannot sleep in the corridor."

"No, but she can stay with us."

Even *I* thought that was a bad idea, but the wheels were already in motion.

CHAPTER SEVEN

The spacious suite seemed to shrink in the presence of two women whose larger-than-life personalities and varying degrees of hostility bordered on the explosive.

Preferring not to ignite the smoldering embers, I deemed it sensible to apply my deductive skills to the problem… elsewhere. Discretion being the better part of valor.

On the ground floor, I sought out my newest best friend. Stepping into the oppressive afternoon heat, I joined Hank at the valet stand for a quick chat.

When he spotted me, Hank flipped open the patrons' key box. Before I could stop him, I noticed the Packard's keys dangling from his hand.

"Heading out, Mr. Butterfield? Give me a minute to bring that powerhouse around—"

"No, Hank, I am not going anywhere, at least not yet, but I wondered whether you had a few moments to spare to give me a hand with something else?"

Hank shot a quick glanced at the hotel entrance. I imagine to see whether our interaction was observed.

"I'll make it worth your while," I sweetened the pot,

pulling a ten-spot from my billfold, and holding it up. His eyes bulged. It was probably more than he made in tips shuffling people's cars around.

I let him snatch it and stuff it in his pocket. *He was my fish, now.*

"What do you need?"

"Mr. Brigmann."

At the mention of the man's name, Hank's tanned face, blanched.

He reached into his pocket to retrieve the bill, explaining, "Oh, no. I stay away from that man. I value my health."

"Well, that's good because I'm not asking about him. I'm curious about a woman who came down in the elevator earlier."

"Floppy hat, sunglasses, and more makeup than the Max Factor Corporation?" he said somewhat snootily.

Clearly, his opinion of her was not high.

"That's the one." I nodded.

"She's one of the fan dancers who perform in the night club."

"Any idea of her name?"

"Her stage name, well kinda. It's as fake as her French accent, Fifi LeFleur or something ridiculous like that."

Aware that Hank knew the make, model, and, probably, serial number of every guest's vehicle. I ventured, "Do you know what she drives?"

"Who doesn't? It was all the buzz when she arrived in it. 1940 Lincoln Continental Cabriolet. Beautiful maroon paint job. Word has it, Mr. Brigmann bought it for her."

"Does she keep it in valet parking?"

"Not even she gets that luxury. If she's here, you'll find it in the employees' parking lot. Now you mention her, I guess dancing naked doesn't pay as much as you'd think," he mused, tapping his lips,

"Why do you say that?" I had known prostitutes in the past… and how much they could make during the night… but had not made the acquaintance of any exotic dancers, so their *income* remained an enigma.

"A couple of days ago, I saw her coming out of House-keeping."

"You think she was looking for more work?"

"Who knows? She was probably there to bitch about the condition of her dressing room. Of course, you did not hear this from me."

"Nope… we were just discussing the scratch you put on my wife's car."

"A **scratch**?"

I left Hank babbling about that being an impossibility and last saw him running towards the garage to verify my complaint. Bless him.

Approaching the employee parking lot, I noted it was under the watchful eye of a security guard… *interesting*. This level of protection for the casino made me ponder whether manage-ment trusted anyone.

A group of employees were heading to and from the lot. It must be a shift change. Most still wore their dealers' uniforms, but some were in street clothes. Regardless, each one was stopped by the guard, who requested to see inside the women's bags and asked the men to turn out their pockets.

A second group came out, who might well provide me with access to the automobiles.

One by one, the employees presented their purses and pockets to the guard. Their faces did not seem to warrant anything other than a cursory glance, the guard was more interested in ensuring they were not concealing casino contraband as they left.

I joined the queue, and when my turn came, the guard paused, and took a second to look at my face. Striving to appear relaxed, I summoned up a casual smile, hoping I looked confident. I held my breath, but whatever he saw satisfied him and he waved me on.

In the parking lot, I scanned the rows of vehicles. Picking out the conspicuous, maroon Lincoln was a piece of cake, it stood out like a queen on a throne.

Approaching the Cabriolet nonchalantly, I was thankful Miss LeFleur had seen fit to leave the top of the convertible down.

Standing next to the driver's side door, I checked my surroundings then dropped the sun visor, noting the vehicle was registered to one Dottie Green... *so much for being French*... who lived in the township of Henderson.

I flipped the visor up, as an angry voice demanded, "Hey, you, get away from that car. You can't be here. Who the hell are you?"

Plastering on a shocked expression, I exclaimed, "This is not my green Chevy coupe." I brushed past the security guard. "Wait, don't think this is even my apartment's parking lot." Hotfooting it out before the man could catch me.

Back in the hotel, I stopped at one of their courtesy phones to place a long-distance call to an old friend.

"Captain Louis Mazzetti. How may I help you?"

"You sounded like a real cop, Lou." I chuckled.

"Christ, I should have known it was you, Butters. After

the call I got from that Detective Harrington, I knew it was only a matter of time before I heard your annoying voice. Can I assume I need to bail you out of the clink?"

"Hardly, Lou. Besides, I have an entire legal team to keep me out of trouble."

"And a wife with more money than sense doesn't hurt either."

"You're just jealous, my friend."

"Look, Jake, some of us have to work for a living, so get to the point or I'm hanging up."

"Fine. Anyone ever tell you you're a bore to talk to."

"Yeah, my wife every night. I'm hanging up now."

"Wait, wait. I need you to run a records check on a dame."

"Who the hell am I, your secretary?" Mazzetti groused.

"Honest, Lou, I wouldn't ask if it wasn't important."

"Is this to help Fitzhugh?"

I heard him choke over Stella's name. Those two were definitely oil and water.

"Her name is Russo now, and yes."

"I couldn't care less if her name is Mary Magdalene. Give me one good reason why I should go out of my way for that extortionist, and just permanently rid myself of her by letting the state of Nevada gas her with cyanide?"

"Because that's not you, Lou. You couldn't live with yourself if you did." I was not sure whether that evaluation of my former partner was true… but it was worth a shot.

Silence filled the line, but when I heard his long-suffering sigh, I gave a silent cheer.

"Give me the details and call me back in a couple of hours. And, Butters…"

"Yeah?"

"This makes us even. No more favors."

"You have my word, Lou. At this point, we're square."

While waiting to call Mazzetti back, I did a little snooping around the theater lounge area of the casino. Poking my head through a side entrance by the stage, I saw the show-girls practicing their routines. Some were in full costume, others were… well… not.

One of the girls, dressed as though she had just popped out of a birthday cake, elbowed her way past me on her way in.

Hoping she did not retaliate with a knuckle sandwich to my face, I snagged her arm. "Excuse me, is Miss LeFleur here?"

Her derisory huff gave me the impression it was a question she had heard far too often from the fan dancer's admirers, as she tried to shrug off my hand with a growled warning, "Kindly release me before I call security."

I relaxed my grip.

"As for her majesty, you'll find her there in the corner, by herself, of course." She flicked her hand.

We looked at the woman, bathed in the glow of a spot-light, fluttering feathered covered fans, and yelling at anyone who breathed in her direction.

I studied her features, imprinting them into my brain in order to describe her to Stella, hoping she was lucid enough during Red's murder to recall what the housemaid looked like.

The dancer cautioned, "If I were you, bud, I would *not* bother her. She's spoken for by a very nasty man. Mind, given their personalities, I am not sure which is worse."

When I did not respond immediately, she shook her head and walked away. "Your funeral."

By the time I turned to thank her, she had vanished into the dimly lit lounge.

My focus strayed to the various spotlights illuminating the dancers on stage, and something Stella mentioned in her story occurred to me.

As silently as possible, and trying not to bump into anything, considering the darkness of the lounge, I made my way up to the lighting booth.

I peered through one of the windows, spying a young fella with a set of headphones clamped over his ears, playing around with several switches, stopping occasionally to jot down a note. I supposed he was in the middle of choreographing the spectacle.

Gently, then more firmly, I rapped on the door to get his attention. His irritated expression indicated I had succeeded.

Yanking the door open, he snarled, "How the hell do you lot expect me to do my job if all you do is bother me?"

I knew he would not be able to see my ID properly, so I flashed it which elicited a frustrated eye roll.

"Christ, another cop."

He said it. I did not. So, no impersonating a policeman in my book. "Name's, Butterfield."

"Yeah, yeah… like I told your friends, the power outage was not caused by the cheap wiring in this place."

"How would you know that?"

"Do you guys ever talk to each other, or are you too busy shoving donuts in your mouths?"

"Look, just humor me." I tried not to laugh at his stereotyping.

"Will that mean I can finish my job?"

"I promise, I won't bother you again. How about we start with your name?"

"Jackson. Write it down so you'll remember it. Anyway, I double as the resort's maintenance guy."

"You must make a decent income, having two important jobs."

"Hardly, all work and no pay. Anyway, when I get this note from someone upstairs telling me they want to test the elevator to the penthouse, and they would make it worth my while if I did it at a specific time, who am I to refuse?"

"If they were just testing the elevators, why would the penthouse be affected?" The question was so obvious, but I felt inclined to ask.

Jackson snorted. "That's what I was told to do, so I did it. Now, if you don't mind, I have four hours to orchestrate five hours' worth of staging."

Without waiting for an answer, he banged the door shut.

A glance at my brand new Omega Seamaster wristwatch, a gift from Pamela who refused to tell me how she procured one before its official release, told me I should probably call Lou.

Coming across a bank of payphone booths, I decided privacy was worth a handful of nickels.

The call went through and Mazzetti did not even bother to offer a greeting.

"Your Green woman has a rap sheet here in California dating back to 1935. Spent time in juvie for petty theft, then graduated to writing bad checks and fraud. There's an outstanding bench warrant for her arrest in Hollywood. Seems she's missed some court dates. If you have any idea where she is, I'm sure you could score some points with the Hollywood PD by cluing them in."

"I appreciate the help, Lou. I'll bring you a souvenir from Sin City."

"Yeah, yeah," he replied. "Stay out of trouble. I don't need any more calls from Homicide there."

"I promise, mom." I chuckled, and was about to hang up, when he said,

"Jake…" there was a pause, "tell Pamela I said *hey…* and Stella, too."

I think that was the first time Lou had been anything other than dismissive towards Stella since I've known the pair.

"Will do. See you when we get back."

CHAPTER EIGHT

The table I had selected for the upcoming entertainment was in the middle of the lounge. Close enough for Stella to get a good look at the dancers but concealed by the spotlights so they could not see us.

Even with my careful preparations, the two women complained about my choice of show.

"Jacob, we could have gone to *any* other venue on the Strip. Why, in God's name, did you insist on this one?"

Stella chimed in, "I have to agree with Pammie…"

What had happened in the hotel room while I was absent to prompt the diminutive?

"…this has to be the worst of the worst… and I hired most of them."

I had not told either about my plan because I did not want to influence Stella's possible identification of Dottie Green.

"Come on, you two. Give them a chance. You might find it interesting."

"Jacob Butterfield."

I thought I was about to get a tongue lashing from Pamela, startled when it came from Stella.

"If your wife and I want to see naked women, we can stand into front of the mirr—"

The lights dimmed and the orchestra filled the lounge with jazz tunes. The combination did wonders to silence them. With matching and marked reluctance, they settled back and drank their martinis.

For the first half an hour, the stage was clogged with scantily clad women adorned in sequins and rhinestones. I could hear Stella grumbling under her breath, "Clods. The lot of them. That's not how I arranged it. For heaven's sake, Louise, can't you walk down the stairs without looking like one of the Three Stooges?"

Ordering a second round of drinks, Pamela nudged Stella in an attempt to curb the latter's complaints about the dancers, whispering, "No sense drawing attention to us. I'm betting there's a reason Jake is making us suffer through this."

Biting her tongue, Stella gulped down the drink the moment it reached the table, a past master, sorry… mistress, at holding her alcohol — unlike Pamela. My wife was on her third by the time the parade of showgirls exited the stage. All the lights went black, except a single spotlight trained on the slit between the curtains.

The orchestra's music changed to something I could only describe as instrumental salaciousness. The saxophones sounded as though they were cavorting in the pit, with the trumpets in bawdy pursuit.

A clear indication, the next act was the featured entertainment.

A voice blared through the speakers, "Ladies and Gentlemen. The Platinum Empire Lounge is proud to present the one and only, direct from Paris, Miss Fifi LeFleur."

A smattering of applause rippled through the yet to be impressed crowd, and a couple of drunks hollered their approval. Unfortunately, one of them was my normally sophisticated wife.

Before I jumped in where angels fear to tread by mentioning this, a stocking-clad leg poked out from the curtain, the foot encased in a stiletto heel. As it planted on the stage, a brilliant, white, circular fan slipped from behind the curtain and fluttered in place.

The orchestra began a slow crescendo, ever louder and higher. As the music continued its ascent, the curtains parted gradually… inch by tantalizing inch until the orchestra reached an ear-splitting peak and all was revealed.

In the middle of an otherwise empty stage, two enormous Burlesque feather fans fluttered, masking the performer's identity. The main ceiling spotlight faded, replaced by a smaller beam behind the dancer, sending interesting shadows across the stage.

Pamela's hoots were getting louder, and Stella was no help, plying her with more cocktails because she thought it was a riot to watch my wife toss her inhibitions to the four winds.

The fan dancer continued her performance unfazed by the shenanigans at our table. She swayed provocatively, swirling the white plumes in a dizzying display, ensuring one always camouflaged her while the other was tossed in abstract arcs. She twirled on her toes, pirouetting like a butterfly until the rhythm slowed and the music dwindled.

The fans fluttered, separating to expose a woman clad in a flesh-colored leotard.

The audience applauded as she bowed and left the stage.

I watched for Stella's reaction, which was not long in coming. The glass she was trying to pry out of Pamela's hands shattered when Stella pounded it on the table. It was only my quick reflexes which prevented her rushing head-long onto the stage. Given the judge's remarks, we did *not* need a charge of assault being brought against Stella, however justifiable.

"Stella, don't go strangling the woman." Her frustrated hiss affirming my assumption. "We need to find out how she fits into this before you settle your score."

"Which part?" she snapped. "The part where she was sleeping with my husband or the part where she is trying to frame me for murder?"

"Hopefully both," I said flatly. "For now, let's use your influence to get backstage and have a quiet chat."

One of the security guards considered barring our entry through the stage door, until Stella pinned him with a look, letting him know such a denial would cost him, at the very least, his job at the Platinum Empire, at most… that did not bear thinking about.

Prudently, he stood aside.

We followed the corridor past several dressing rooms. The door to the largest, set up for the showgirls, was wide open. The women inside appeared unconcerned whether anyone saw them changing or standing around naked.

A door at the far end of the hall on the left bore a star, and a name scrawled in black: Fifi LeFleur. We had reached the fan dancer's dressing room.

I knocked. "Miss LeFleur?"

From the other side of the door, I heard a chair scrape against the floor, and a pair of heels tap-tap across the room.

In an affected French accent straight from a movie screen, came, "Oo ees eet?"

Pamela giggled. "Fans of your fans."

Stella clapped her hand on Pamela's mouth and dragged her behind me, so Fifi would not see them clearly.

The door opened onto the, unexpectedly, petite dancer. She sent me a queer look, possibly wondering how we had gained admission to an area off limits to the public.

Bestowing on us a smile as phony as her accent, she cooed, "Though I appreciate meeting fans, I do not 'ave time to sign autographs. Forgive me, I must prepare for my next show."

"That's okay," I replied. "I'm not here for Miss LeFleur's signature. Perhaps I ought to introduce myself. My name is Jacob Butterfield, and I am a private investigator, here to question Dottie Green about a murder."

Grasping her shoulders, I pushed her backwards before she could shut the door in my face. Stella ushered Pamela in, and turned the key in the lock.

Stepping out from my shadow, Stella demanded, "Ok, you little whore, what were you doing in my bedroom? Having sex with my husband, or were you there to murder him? Tell me now before I tear out your fake blonde hair by its dark roots and wring your scrawny neck with it."

"I-I do not know of what you speak," Dottie tried to demur, deliberately emphasising her artificial French inflexion. This affectation proved the last straw for Stella who landed a solid backhand across her cheek.

"Dammit, bitch," Dottie squawked in a distinctly Midwestern twang and rubbed the quickly darkening palm print.

"Unless you want another one, spill," Stella's ice-cold tone was far more intimidating than her temper.

I pressed what I hoped was a calming hand on Stella's arm and intervened, giving her the opportunity to compose herself, and allowing me to get a word in edgewise. "Miss

Green, unless you want me to let Mrs. Russo pummel you to death, I suggest you tell her what she wants to know."

"I'm telling you, I don't know anything. I wasn't in the penthouse. I'm a performer, not a maid."

"Bullshit," I heard the expletive erupt behind me.

We all looked at Stella.

"I'd recognize those two assets of yours anywhere, girl, with or without clothes."

Pamela tried to shush her, to get a, "Well, I could," for her efforts.

Shaking my head, I faced the dancer. "Currently, you have two options. You can either tell me the truth about what happened in the penthouse, after which I will turn my back and let you walk…" I paused to let that sink in.

"Or?" she pried warily.

"Or, I drop a nickel to Hollywood PD and let them know where to find you."

Her expression told me that whatever she was wanted for back in California would result in a lengthy sojourn in Tehachapi, the women's prison.

Who knows, she and Vanessa, Pamela's sister, might become bosom friends.

Dottie's frantic gaze met Stella's outraged glare over my shoulder. "Please, Mrs. Russo, you have to believe me. I had nothing to do with your husband's death. I admit, I was sent up to the penthouse to seduce him. I figured someone was gonna show up and take some embarrassing pictures.

"When I arrived, he was busy in his office. I went into the bedroom to wait for him and stripped… ya know as a surprise."

"Did you have sex?" It was Pamela who voiced the accusation.

"No, I swear. I heard the phone ring, and he was arguing with someone named Cohen."

Of course, everyone in Vegas knew who Eli Cohen was but Dottie had decided, in her precarious position, to play dumb.

"Then you arrived, Mrs. Russo. I heard you two bickering, and you threatened him. I got dressed because, by then, luring him into bed seemed like a waste of time, although I'm pretty good, even if I do say so myself."

"Jacob," Stella's voice was strained. "Let me kill her and be done with it."

The woman's eyes widened in panic. "P-Please, Mr. Butterfield, that's all I know."

"Where were you when the lights went out?" I pressed her for more information.

"I was coming out of the bedroom. I had just reached the office when I saw the flashes of the gun's barrel. The lights came back on, the gun was in Mrs. Russo's lap, and Mr. Russo was sprawled across his desk. I did what any sane person would do and screamed until Aristo… I mean Mr. Brigmann… held a pistol against the back of Mrs. Russo's head and told me to call the police."

"Did you actually see her fire the pistol?" I asked.

"How the hell was I supposed to do that? The lights were out."

"Is there anything else you can think of? Something you might have seen in Brigmann's hotel room?"

"I-I have never been—"

"Your brand-new burgundy Lincoln says otherwise, Miss Green."

"All I know is he keeps a bunch of papers there."

A knock at the door accompanied by a, "Miss LeFleur, you're on in fifteen," prompted Dottie to sink onto a stool in front of a mirror and begin covering the bruising caused by Stella's hand. "You heard him. If there's nothing else, please leave," she beseeched.

Disappointed at being thwarted in her desire to punch Dottie Green's lights out, Stella unlocked the door and led Pamela into the hall.

In my best police detective voice I said, "If I was you, Miss Green, I would forget about the next show and clear out pronto. Shit's about to hit the fan," I did not soften my language, needing Dottie to understand the gravity of her situation, "and I doubt you'll want to be here when it does."

"That's the difference between us, Butterfield."

"What?"

"You're not me and can leave whenever you want. Now, if you don't mind."

Shutting the door with a soft click, I swore I heard the exotic dancer sobbing.

CHAPTER NINE

"Christ, Butters," Stella lamented, as I concentrated on picking the lock to Aristo Brigmann's suite. "Do you have arthritis or something in your old age? It never took you this long when *we* were together. I'm guessing you've become too accustomed to this fat cat lifestyle."

I glanced over my shoulder to see her send Pamela an accusatory glare. My wife smiled sweetly and flipped her the bird.

I sniped, "That was out of necessity. You were a terrible lookout."

No sooner had the words left my mouth, did the lock spring free, and the door creaked open. I was hit in the face by the stench of stale cigar smoke, cheap perfume, and sex.

Whatever happened in this room, besides fronting the Eastern Syndicate's sponsorship of the resort, was something to which I did not wish to be privy.

As neat and tidy as Brigmann appeared to the outside world, the interior of his suite revealed the real man. It was a mess, papers strewn everywhere.

I thought my filing system was unrivaled.

As we entered, Stella kicked a stray ice bucket by the door. A chunk of ice and half a bucket of water spilled onto the carpet, along with an empty champagne bottle and a lethal-looking ice pick.

"Shit," she growled. "We better find something incriminating because there's no hiding someone was here. Brigmann is no fool, he'll put two and two together and come up with fifteen."

"Just watch your big feet," a sobered Pamela cautioned, adding, her tone slightly rattled, "What sort of ice do you get here in Vegas? That could do some serious damage." She indicated the pick.

Stella shuddered at the images *that* elicited.

"Never mind the ice-pick. Check this out," I waved at the desk, reminding them of our purpose. We sifted through the papers littering the surface and, almost immediately, discovered Brigmann's duplicity, clarifying why he needed a fall guy or, in this case, gal.

Every invoice stamped as *PAID*, had a duplicate, but the pricing on the second copy was twenty to thirty percent higher.

"Holy hell." I whistled incredulously. "Brigmann is cooking the books. Over-billing the mob, no less. No wonder Cohen thought Russo was squandering money."

Pamela, thumbing through another stack of documents realized it was correspondence between the contractors and the hotel. She handed a few to Stella. "Have you seen any of these?"

Stella scanned them, her eyes widening. "No wonder we couldn't get the contractors to show up. This asshole was either shortchanging them or cancelling them all together. So, although the mob sent Brigmann to rein it in, he made it worse... deliberately."

"I would not say worse," a clipped European voice jerked

our attention to the door where Aristo Brigmann stood, gun in one hand, the other gripping Dottie Green by her elbow.

Shoving the dancer into one of the chairs, and without taking his eyes off us, Brigmann ordered, "Sit there, bitch. I'll deal with your betrayal when I'm done with these three.

"Kindly replace those documents, you interfering nuisances." He paused. "On second thoughts, my argument that I found you rifling through my private files after breaking into my room, might hold more weight if you die with said papers clutched in your grimy paws."

Before I could react, he fired. The bullet sliced straight through the sheaf I was holding and into my shoulder. I bit down on a crude profanity, my hand spasmed, and the stack fluttered to the floor as I dropped like a stone.

Pamela shrieked, "Jacob. Oh, my God. You've killed him."

In pain, but coherent, I deduced Brigmann thought himself an expert marksman and, thanks in no small part to my wife's theatrics, probably assumed he had fired a fatal shot. I heard him say coldly, "Don't worry, Mrs. Butterfield, you'll be joining your husband shortly.

"First, if you don't mind, take the gun from your husband's ankle holster. Despite my source in the Vegas police assuring me that the esteemed Detective Harrington had confiscated your husband's peashooter, no gumshoe worth their salt gives up all their weapons willingly."

Pamela glanced down at me. Our eyes connected for the briefest instant, then she looked at my ankle. "Why? So, I can shoot you for killing my husband?"

"Not me, Russo." He swung the gun in Stella's direction. For dragging you into this farce." A devious grin spread across his face, "The police will call it justifiable retribution." He sounded like the devil offering Pamela a deal she could not possibly reject.

Cocking the hammer, he reiterated, "Now, be a good girl and do as you're told. The gun."

Kneeling, and with perfect timing, Pamela pushed my pant leg up. In a split second, I had withdrawn the .32 from its holster and, ignoring the agony spearing down my arm, fired two rounds.

One produced a rather interesting bright red stain on his white shirt, but the second missed entirely, burrowing into the plaster wall behind him.

Brigmann's pistol slipped out of his fist as he stumbled backwards, landing heavily on the carpet.

Curiously, next to where I had shot him, a tiny red pinprick bloomed while, beneath him, the puddle of blood expanded like a bloody halo.

Dottie Green, no longer cowed and compliant in her chair, was standing over Brigmann, his gun gripped in her trembling hands.

"I warned you not to touch me, Ari, but noooo," she drew out the word, her fury a tangible thing, "you could not resist hurting me, you bastard. You could have let me go."

Later, I discovered Dottie had taken advantage of the chaos to seize the icepick and plunge it into Brigmann as he staggered from the gunshot. The stiletto point had entered his back between the fourth and fifth ribs, straight into his heart.

The added pressure caused by the suddenness of his fall combined with the weight of his body on impact with the floor, forced the vicious steel tip right through, resulting in the second, albeit minute, perforation to the skin on his chest.

According to the coroner, it was a one-in-a-million puncture.

Clearly, it was not Aristo Brigmann's day.

I risked an approach to relieve Dottie of the weapon, but she brandished it at me, wildly.

"Don't take another step, Butterfield. I'll kill you too if I have to."

Raising one of my palms in defense, I said as calmly as possible, "We're not going to hurt you, Dottie. Give me the gun and let the police handle the rest."

"In this town? Are you kidding? I'm as good as dead if I do." She swiped Brigmann's stuffed wallet from the inside pocket of his linen jacket. A quick check seemed to satisfy her. "I'm outta here. Don't you dare follow me."

"Don't worry, Dottie, you are the least of my concerns, but before you skedaddle, would you mind telling us what happened after we left you?"

She hesitated, clearly torn between absconding and driving the ice pick, figuratively, deeper into Ari's heart.

"Please," I wheedled, "it's vital we have the whole picture."

"Ok, but then I'm gone."

"Agreed." I motioned to Pamela and Stella to stay where they were so as not to alarm Dottie any further. As her rage subsided, she seemed to deflate, shrink almost… possibly in relief her nightmare was almost over.

Grudgingly, she handed me the pistol, sank into a chair, and filled in the last gap of the sordid tale.

Dottie's Story

As transcribed by Pamela Butterfield, to the best of her recollection, in the wake of Brigmann's death.

After we left her, Dottie Green considered the ramifications of her actions. Her thoughts were interrupted by a second knock on her door.

It was the stage manager. "You go on in five."

Dottie called out, "Hey, Malcolm, can you announce the cancellation of the next show?"

"Is there anything wrong? Should I get the casino medical staff?" A lofty term which actually referred to a doctor of questionable accreditation, and even worse skill.

"No, but I twisted my ankle during the last show. I thought icing it might help, but no luck. I think I'm gonna call it and head home."

She heard a key jiggle in the lock, forgetting Malcolm possessed the master keys to the dressing rooms.

His running joke had always been, "You can't tell when some performer is gonna die on stage… and then, literally, in their dressing room."

Dottie opened her dresser drawer, propped her right foot on it, and covered her ankle with a convenient a towel before Malcolm came in.

He frowned at the sight. "Ya mind if I take a look?"

"Yeah, kinda. It really hurts."

"You know the boss ain't gonna like you skipping out of your next show."

"I don't see why it matters. There were barely enough people at the last show to fill a handful of tables, and that's being generous. If not for the drunks, I could have been entertaining mannequins."

"Fine, but you ain't getting paid for the next show."

"Oh, damn," she bemoaned sarcastically. "Guess I won't be retiring tonight."

She rose to her feet, faking a hobble, and the stage manager asked, "You gonna make it out to your car, or shall I get Wally to help you?"

Given Wally was anything but graceful and would probably end up actually hurting her, she shook her head. "Nah, I reckon I can manage if I go slow."

"Your call," he said carelessly, and left the room, closing

the door behind him. Knowing someone would catch hell from Brigmann, Malcolm hurried to the public address microphone.

"Ladies and Gentlemen, the Platinum Empire is sorry to announce Miss Fifi LeFleur's next performance has been cancelled due to injury. In her place, an encore presentation of the musical stylings of Victoria Jennings."

Dottie muttered, "Only if you can drag her away from the buffet table."

Satisfied her absence was covered for the time being, she grabbed an oversized garment bag and cleared out her dressing table. Clothes, makeup, wigs, everything was shoved in tightly to make room for more.

Dropping the last of her lipsticks into the bag, Dottie hooked it onto her arm, and opened the door. Checking that the corridor was clear, she shut the door quietly and headed for the employee parking lot.

She never made it.

As she rounded the first corner, a hand fell on her shoulder. She expected it to be Stella Russo waiting to pounce — a far more preferable alternative.

"Where are you off to, doll?" The man's European intonation was evident, even after the years he had spent in the US.

"A-Ari," Dottie spluttered. "W-what are you doing down here?"

"Imagine my concern when I heard our star performer, not to mention, my girl, had to cancel one of her shows because she had injured herself. I rushed over thinking I ought to take you to the Emergency Room, to find you carrying a bag like Santa Claus without so much as a limp. You must have superhuman recuperative powers."

Under Aristo's vice-like grip, pain radiated from Dottie's shoulder all the way to her wrist.

"Come up to my room, where I can examine your ankle."

"I-it's alright, Ari, really. I'm just gonna go home and—" She grimaced and fell silent when his nails dug into her skin.

He forced her to the elevators. Leaning in, he whispered into her ear menacingly, "No, my dear, I insist, and will not take no for an answer."

"You know the rest," she finished miserably.

We sat in silence, letting her words sink in. Stabbing Brigmann aside, nothing he did not deserve, she was a very lucky girl.

"You're safe now," Pamela said, quietly. "It was a brave thing you did, took guts."

Dottie's pallid features looked less pinched.

Stella did not speak, but her stance had relaxed… marginally.

Familiar with her body language, *do not tell Pamela*, I exhaled slowly. "One other thing." I handed Brigmann's gun to Dottie. "You might need this, sooner or later."

She stared at me for a moment, then nodded and accepted the pistol. I could never be sure, but I thought I saw her mouth *Thank You* as she fled.

The aforementioned Detective Harrington stood in the cluttered room, watching the men in white removing Brigmann's body. He scratched his head under his hat, trying to comprehend what he had been told.

"Let me get this straight," he said for, at least, the fourth time. "Brigmann invited you up to his suite to discuss buying

Mrs. Russo out of the casino's partnership, enabling her to afford a decent lawyer to prove her innocence, with enough left to enjoy a reasonably comfortable life.

"During the meeting, a heavy-set guy, wearing dark clothes, his hat tilted downwards which hid his face, broke into the room, stabbed Brigmann in the back with an ice pick, and shot you in the shoulder.

"You managed to return fire using a pistol you failed to hand over when I asked for your weapons, accidentally hitting Brigmann *after* he was stabbed."

"Yep, clean forgot about the one on my ankle, and that's how it happened." I infused the perfect blend of honesty, shock, pain, and confusion into my reply, while a medic patched up my damaged shoulder, which hurt like the devil. Thankfully, Brigmann's aim was appalling and, although rather nasty, it was only a flesh wound; the bullet had missed the bone completely.

"Sure, it did." Not fooled for an instant, Harrington's eye roll was Stella-worthy. "And where might I ask, is this mysterious assassin?"

"Fled."

"Of course, he did. How convenient," Harrington's skepticism was palpable. "Butterfield…"

"Yes, Detective Harrington?" My expression was the picture of innocence.

"Get your ass out of my city.'

"With pleasure, sir."

CHAPTER TEN

A few days later, my wife and I were in the lobby, to check out when Stella appeared. "What? You two thought you could sneak off without so much as a goodbye?"

Feigning remorse, Pamela replied, "It's a long drive back to San Francisco, and we wanted to get an early start. I'm sure you understand."

Before Stella could answer, four goons in baggy suits approached, flanking a shorter, middle-aged man with black, slicked back hair. His squat stature aside, he exuded power.

I did not need to wait for an introduction to know who he was, and that he was not there to see me. He made a beeline for Stella.

"Ah, Mrs. Russo, permit me to introduce myself, and please forgive my tardiness in doing so." He dipped an old-fashioned bow. "Eli Cohen."

Stella accepted the notorious gangster's outstretched hand, and they shook. "To what do I owe the pleasure, Mr. Cohen?"

"Come now, Stella, do you mind if I call you Stella?" he

asked, his tone respectful. "After everything you have endured these past few weeks, please call me Eli."

Slack-jawed, Pamela and I gawked at this casual introduction.

"Let me apologize for my former accountant's reprehensible conduct against you and your late husband."

"I take responsibility for not keeping a tighter rein on Red, Mr. Coh…"

Cohen canted his head at Stella who blushed slightly and amended, "Eli."

"Mistakes were made by all, I'm afraid. I'm happy to hear that, with the help of these two," he nodded at Pamela and me, "you had the fortitude to correct Brigmann's discrepancies. I believe it was on a par with my own methods."

He gave Stella an approving smile, before slipping his arm around her. The height difference between Stella in her heels and the much shorter Cohen was almost humorous, but not a mouth twitched.

Urging Stella forward, he proposed, "What say we have a drink, and a chat?"

"I would love to, Eli," Stella made sure to address him properly, "but, while we do, might you be so kind as to grant me the use of some of your entourage?"

"Come now, why in the world would you need protection? Be assured, you have nothing to fear from me."

"Oh, heavens no, Eli." Stella jerked her thumb at us. "I want to make sure these two stay put until our business is concluded."

Cohen eyeballed Pamela and me. "Winston, Paul." The two beefiest bodyguards stepped forward. "Keep those two company."

"Aye, Mr. Cohen," one of the guards replied.

"Oh, and Winston."

"Yes, sir?"

"Keep them in one piece or, at least, try to."

With that blatant warning for us to behave, he and Stella disappeared into the casino lounge.

It seemed like an eternity waiting for Stella and Cohen to return. Pamela, tired of standing around, had retreated to one of the wing-back chairs populating the lobby.

When they reappeared, Cohen's features were marred with what resembled disappointment. As they approached, he asked her a question which, from her expression, I guessed he had repeated several times during their conversation.

"I promise you full control for the remainder of the construction, plus a hearty salary upon completion. You would be the first woman in charge of a major casino and hotel anywhere in the world. Plus, I guarantee the full protection of my associates. Are you certain I cannot persuade you to stay?"

"As tempting as your offer is, Eli, in addition to your forgiveness for what transpired upstairs, in good faith, I must decline. Please understand, these unfortunate events have kill—" wincing, she revised that to, "ruined any desire I once had to live in Vegas."

He blew a weighty sigh but maintained his composure. It was obvious his largesse was rarely, if ever, refused… especially by a woman. His look of resignation indicated he respected Stella and was sad to lose her.

"Well, my dear, if you change your mind, you will always have a home here."

"I appreciate that, Eli, more than you know." With characteristic insouciance, Stella brushed a light kiss to his cheek.

A faint flush washed up his face, and he could not quite hide a smile. Bowing in an oddly old fashioned manner, he strode away, signaling for his men to follow.

I was the one who decided to poke the elephant in the room. "Now what?"

"I think I'll return to San Francisco for the time being and take stock. No point in rushing at things."

A frown knitted Pamela's brow.

"Pammie, you wouldn't mind me tagging along, would you? Butters has to drive that hulking great Studebaker, and I'm sure you'd enjoy the company."

Pamela shot me a glare telling me to dissuade Stella's sugges-tion, but I had to admit, it made a lot of sense. I shrugged.

Grasping at straws, Pamela asked, "Don't you have a car?"

"'Fraid not. It belongs to the casino. If it makes you that uncomfortable, Pam, I can hitchhike."

"That ain't gonna happen," Pamela muttered grudgingly. "Go pack your stuff."

"Already have, Hank put it in your trunk." Stella grinned smugly.

Pamela opened her mouth to protest, then gave up, turned and stalked outside to her waiting Packard.

As we drove through the Nevada desert toward Baker, I kept as close as possible to the Packard.

Something told me the ceasefire was not permanent.

Sure enough, wild gesticulations began in the convertible. Whatever the two women were discussing, had taken on the appearance of two volatile Mediterranean types arguing about the price of fruit.

The car slewed across the road, the jerky mime continuing unabated, until Pamela skidded to a stop, got out, and stormed around to the passenger door. With a strength I had no clue she possessed, my wife hauled Stella onto the verge, her fingers snarled through the latter's newly bleached hair.

Clawing at Pamela's hands, Stella attempted to break free. She clocked Pamela in the jaw, which resulted in Pamela dropping Stella face first onto the gravel.

Blood dripping from her nose, the blonde scrambled to her feet, and charged the brunette, tackling her. Dirt kicked up around them as they wrestled.

Pamela landed several brutal, martial arts blows to her opponent's back. Stella responded with whatever tactics she had learned on the streets.

As I drew up alongside, I heard Pamela declare, "The city is too small for both of us," and, "I'm sure as shit you ain't getting my husband,"

Stella crowed snarkily, "If you ain't woman enough to keep him, you don't deserve him."

Concerned the pair would inflict some serious damage on each other, I yanked my recently returned pistol from its holster and fired into the air.

The two skittered, wide-eyed, to opposite ends of the large automobile, glaring at each other like caged tigers, while verifying neither had been hit by the gunshot. Satisfied there were no life-threatening injuries, they directed their fury at the man with his gun pointed in the air.

Now I had their attention, I bellowed, "Enough, both of you. Get a grip and start behaving like goddamned adults."

Sheepishly, they complied.

I infused a gentle note into my voice, "Stella, not long ago, I came across an old saying, something along the lines of, there is a love for a season and a love for a lifetime. It struck a chord with me. Yes, I loved you once but, if we are honest, we knew it was fleeting. I can't deny we had fun and shared some great adventures. I admit, for a long time, I thought we were meant to be, but fate had a different path mapped out. I had to come to terms with that on the San Francisco train platform when I watched you leave on the arm of another man."

I looked at my wife, "Pamela, if you don't believe I love you, tell me now and I'll go, but please know, you are my lifetime."

Pamela flew into my arms, and I swept her off her feet. The ensuing embrace spoke a language all of its own, no other words required. Setting my wife on her feet, I spotted Stella wipe away a tear surreptitiously.

"I'm sure you have your passport somewhere in your luggage. Take the Studebaker and drive to the nearest airport."

"Where do you expect me to go?" she rejoined, her voice heavy with sarcasm.

"Paris. We have an apartment there, overlooking the Eiffel Tower. We only use it occasio—"

"Jacob. No," Pamela protested. "That's our escape."

"Consider this a different kind of escape, one which grants us a peaceful life," I replied. In quick understanding, Pamela acquiesced — albeit grudgingly, and with a baleful mutter.

I handed Stella the keys to the apartment and my car. "I bet Cohen gave you enough money to set you up for a while." A memory nudged me. I paused and studied her speculatively. *Did I dare?* I started to speak then thought better of it.

"What?" Stella knows me too well.

"You know it was Russo who stole that damn diamond," I made it a statement, not a question. I expected Stella to be shocked, for her mouth to fall agape at my bald revelation of Russo's guilt. She shrugged. *Shrugged!*

"Stella?" I did not anticipate the toll her reaction took on me. My faith in her, the faith I had held onto all these years, started to splinter, and a shard of ice slid down my spine. "You *knew*?"

Stella had the grace to blush. "Oh Butters, no. I swear, not then. I would have told you, slapped him, and history would be different." she took pains to reassure. "He confessed later, after we were married. He was proud of it, but it triggered a very *very* bitter row, let me tell you. Not sure I ever forgave him for that… things would…"

She shook her head, and her expression softened in reminiscence. "We did good, you and me. I'm truly sorry I walked out and left you in the lurch."

I stared at her, a raft of what ifs chasing around my head. Then I glanced at Pam and my heart thudded. Our eyes met and we shared a smile. Definitely my forever.

Stella followed my gaze and wilted ever-so slightly. My male ego wanted this reaction to be a recognition of what she threw away in search of a *better life*, but I will never know, and Stella would never admit she allowed herself to be seduced by Carmine Russo's flattery.

Then, being Stella, she masked her feelings, straightened her shoulders, and climbed behind the wheel of the behemoth, which made even her look small.

I swapped the respective luggage between the cars and stood next to Pamela. Stella gave us a brief wave and drove away.

"Shall we go home, my love?" I asked Pamela.

"No, my husband, I want to go for a drive."

"Where to?"

She pointed east. "Somewhere in that direction."

Gotta love her decisiveness.

POSTSCRIPT

With the help of Eli Cohen and the Eastern Syndicate, the Platinum Empire Resort came to fruition, with one of his men installed to run the place.

Six months later, it was raided by the Nevada State Police following complaints from reputable gamblers.

Not even the city's Vice Squad could suppress the incompetence and greed. Subsequently, they lost their gambling license.

The last we heard of Stella Fitzhugh... who applied for citizenship in France and had completed the necessary formalities to revert to her maiden name... she was living the life of Riley.

She had transformed our apartment into a social hotspot for the wealthy and titled, and was being spoiled rotten by a widowed viscount who had a villa in Monte Carlo.

As ever — Stella had landed on her feet.

·　·　·

As for yours truly and his wife… we drove until we ran out of road, ending up somewhere in Florida.

At present, we are unwinding in a reasonably respectable hotel, contemplating a trip to Havana. I had heard on the grapevine, about a casino down there that's up for sale, and when I mentioned it to Pammie, she jumped at the opportunity to own her own gambling den.

My darling wife… so sophisticated.

After all, how much trouble could we get into in Cuba?

RORI BLEU

With a smattering of riverboat pirates and royalty in her
heritage, Rori Bleu's childhood reflected her past.
An interest in fairy tales, myth and legend were as important
as spirited discussions around politics and current affairs —
although some might argue they are one and the same!

A fascination, sparked by listening to Grimm's Fairy Tales at
her grandmother's knee, not only encouraged Rori's passion
for reading, but also steered her into the world of RPG's.
What began as a fun pastime, soon evolved into the creation
of fantastical worlds, but Rori never lost her love of politics
going on to specialise in Governmental History and
Historical Research.

Naturally this means her stories are steeped in historical
accuracy and real-life intrigue. While Rori's love of a happily
ever after means her preferred genre is romance, don't be
surprised if you discover an occasional detour into historical
fiction, thrillers, horror and fantasy.

ROSIE CHAPEL

Rosie Chapel lives in Perth, Australia, with her hubby and two rescue fur babies. When not writing, she loves catching up with friends, burying herself in a book (or three), discovering the wonders of Western Australia, or — and the best — a quiet evening at home with her husband, enjoying a glass of wine and a movie.

Website: www.rosiechapel.com

ALSO BY RORI BLEU

Pineapple Meringue

Imprisoned Hearts

Port of London

Dani's Masquerade

Black Tulips

Ajei's Destiny

Porta Aeternum

The Queen's Heart

Syn *with Matthew Forester*

With Rosie Chapel

Tapestry of Shadows and Light - The Hunters Prequel

Echoes and Illusions - The Hunters: Book 1

Smoke and Mirrors - The Hunters : Book 2

Evie's War

Vindicta

Corrupt Covenant

Lesser of Two Evils

Deadly Incision

Tidbits

The Sela Helsdatter Saga

A Flip of The Coin - Book One

Conceived Chaos - Book Two

Odin's Bane - Book Three

Valhalla's Doom - Book Four

Arcane Alchemy: Freya's Fate - *A Helsdatter Saga Novella*

ALSO BY ROSIE CHAPEL

<u>Historical Fiction</u>

The Hannah's Heirloom Sequence

The Pomegranate Tree - Book One

Echoes of Stone and Fire - Book Two

Embers of Destiny - Book Three

Etched in Starlight - Prequel

Hannah's Heirloom Trilogy - Compilation — e-book only

Prelude to Fate

Legacy of Flame and Ash

The Nettleby Trilogy (WW1 Novellas)

A Guardian Unexpected - Book One

Under the Clock - Book Two

Between Heartbeats - Book Three

<u>Regency Romances</u>

The Linen and Lace Series

Once Upon An Earl - Book One

To Unlock Her Heart - Book Two

Love on a Winter's Tide - Book Three

A Love Unquenchable - Book Four

A Hidden Rose — Book Five

An Unexpected Romance

Elusive Hearts - Book One

Shrouded Hearts - Book Two

The Daffodil Garden

The Unconventional Duchess

Rescuing Her Knight - *the de Wiltons:* Book One

His Fiery Hoyden

A Regency Duet

A Regency Christmas Double

Fate is Curious

A Christmas Prayer *with Ashlee Shades*

The Lady's Wager

Winning Emma

A Love Impossible

Unravelling Roana

Love Kindled

Moonbeams and Mistletoe

The Baron's Inheritance

<u>Fairy Tale Romance</u>

Chasing Bluebells

<u>Contemporary Romances</u>

Of Ruins and Romance

All At Once It's You

Cobweb Dreams

Just One Step

His Heart's Second Sigh

With Rori Bleu

Tapestry of Shadows and Light - The Hunters Prequel

Echoes and Illusions - The Hunters: Book 1

Smoke and Mirrors - The Hunters : Book 2

Evie's War

Vindicta

Corrupt Covenant

Lesser of Two Evils

Deadly Incision

Tidbits

The Sela Helsdatter Saga

A Flip of The Coin - Book One

Conceived Chaos - Book Two

Odin's Bane - Book Three

Valhalla's Doom - Book Four

Arcane Alchemy: Freya's Fate - *A Helsdatter Saga Novella*